Rosemary Friedman has published nineteen bestselling novels which have been serialized on BBC radio and widely translated, as have her many short stories. She is a television and screenplay writer and the author of two successful stage plays. She has served on the executive committees of English PEN and the Society of Authors and has judged several literary prizes. She is married to a psychiatrist and lives in London.

PARIS SUMMER

Judith Flatland, together with her two children, leaves Boston and her work at the Museum of Fine Arts, to follow her husband, Jordan, to Paris, where he is about to finalize a high-profile business deal. Bored with her role as 'corporate wife', and suddenly aware that she has become sexually invisible, forty-two-year-old Judith is jealous of her nubile daughter and feels that life is passing her by. Unable to help herself, she is drawn into a passionate affair with Félix Dumoulin, an urbane young artist. What begins as curiosity on her part and a bizarre wager on Félix's, turns into a cataclysm . . .

*Books by Rosemary Friedman
Published by The House of Ulverscroft:*

PROOFS OF AFFECTION
ROSE OF JERICHO
TO LIVE IN PEACE
THE LONG HOT SUMMER
THE LIFE SITUATION
AN ELIGIBLE MAN

ROSEMARY FRIEDMAN

PARIS SUMMER

Complete and Unabridged

ULVERSCROFT
Leicester

First published in Great Britain in 2004 by
Robert Hale Limited
London

First Large Print Edition
published 2005
by arrangement with
Robert Hale Limited
London

British Library CIP Data

Friedman, Rosemary
    Paris summer.—Large print ed.—
    Ulverscroft large print series: romance
    1. Americans—France—Paris—Fiction
    2. Married women—France—Paris—Fiction
    3. Love stories 4. Large type books
    I. Title
    823.9′14 [F]

    ISBN 1–84395–723–X

Published by
F. A. Thorpe (Publishing)
Anstey, Leicestershire

Set by Words & Graphics Ltd.
Anstey, Leicestershire
Printed and bound in Great Britain by
T. J. International Ltd., Padstow, Cornwall

This book is printed on acid-free paper

For Linda Seifert and Elizabeth Dench

Thanks are due to Adrian George, Daniel Green, Edward Kelly, Jane and Harvey Spack, Barnaby Spiro, Plum Le Tan, Renée Tata, Helen Kirk, Dennis Friedman, and the city of Paris.

1

My name is Judith Flatland, I am forty-two years old, raised in New York and domiciled in Boston, no distinguishing features, and I have always feared the elements and been afraid of natural phenomena. Being a human being is pretty scary. I don't mean not having enough to eat, being sick, ill, disadvantaged or living below the poverty line — all these things are bad enough, appalling — but simply having to cope in a world in which every day, from the moment one opens one's eyes, there are a hundred different decisions to be made; each one perhaps unimportant in the grand order of things but determining the path one is to tread and leaving an indelible stamp upon one's life, altering its course.

Most people are scared but manage to hide it. Scared of their insignificance in the cosmos with its seemingly immense past and its incomprehensible future in which, if we are to believe the latest quasi-scientific reports from think-tanks and market researchers who attempt to paint a picture of what life will be like in the twenty-first century, marriage will decline, women will spend less time having families and forming relationships, we can expect to live for around 120 years and there will be a radical restructuring of the traditional timetable of our lives. Given the inadequacy of our physical and mental equipment in the face of the forces we come up against, being scared is hardly surprising. We are born alone and we die alone. We bring nothing with us and we leave with our suitcases empty. It doesn't sound difficult. But it is. There are too many tadpoles in the human pond, too many organisms struggling for survival against odds that most statisticians would find overwhelming. Ants in an ant colony, we struggle along, huddling together for protection, until a boot comes down decimating our busy procession, leaving us to reform and continue the march to the last syllable of recorded time, abandoning our dead behind us. It needn't be a boot. Sometimes it's a broom diverting us from our chosen path (more chance than Darwin), damaging us with its bristles. Or a deluge of water. Cold from the watering-can of natural selection or boiling hot from the kettle of destiny. Still we manage to march on. The survivors.

Once I was in San Francisco. Jordan was downstairs in a postprandial meeting. West Coast bankers. I was performing my ablutions preparatory to going to bed when the

2

water in one of the twin wash-basins started to slop from side to side and the marble tiles trembled beneath my bare feet. It only lasted a few seconds. A tremor, when the earthquake I dreaded and which was never far from my mind, almost became reality. When Jordan came to bed, flushed from the brandy that had been consumed, he said he hadn't noticed anything, too busy with hostile takeover bids and suchlike, it often happened, think nothing of it.

An earthquake is produced by a sudden breaking of rock in the earth's crust as the stresses become too great for the strength of the rock to withstand. Where the rock breaks, a fracture line, known as a fault, is left, and future movements are likely to happen along the same weakness. The force with which the rock breaks releases a large amount of energy in the form of waves that travel through the earth. These waves radiate outwards from where the fault has ruptured. The place at which the rupture begins is known as the hypocentre; the point on the earth's surface directly above the hypocentre is called the epicentre, and the magnitude of the earthquake — the dreaded Richter scale — is a logarithmic approximation of the energy released. Controlling such enormous forces — which claimed 200,000 Chinese lives in

1920 and another 242,000 fifty-six years later, which wreaked indiscriminate havoc from Algeria to Guatemala and, in living memory, much nearer to home when the Northridge earthquake caused major damage to Los Angeles property and entire sections of the freeways collapsed — seems to be out of the question. It is necessary to look at other strategies, such as prediction and earthquake resistant design, to prevent further calamities.

Protecting against volcanoes, in which timely evacuation rather than reinforced buildings is the best option, is another matter. In the simplest terms, a volcano is a vent at the earth's surface where molten rock — magma — from the interior can reach the surface. The magma originates in the mantle, but it is often stored in a magma reservoir with the crust as it moves upwards. It then erupts either as a stream of liquid rock (called lava at the surface) or as ash or cinder. Active volcanoes are those that are currently erupting, a process which can go on intermittently for years; dormant volcanoes may not have erupted for tens or hundreds of years but may be expected to erupt again; while those which were once active in response to the tectonic situation as it was millions of years ago but no longer represent a danger, are said to be extinct.

Catastrophic and disastrous as earthquakes and volcanoes can be, sometimes they give rise to another phenomenon that can cause even more destruction and loss of life: the tsunami. Tsunami is a Japanese word meaning 'harbour wave', or — inaccurately for tides play no part — 'tidal wave'. When an earthquake occurs offshore, it may bring about a sudden change in the shape of the ocean floor. This change causes a massive displacement of water, which in turn produces a powerful wave — or series of waves — that spreads out in all directions. As long as the wave travels in deep ocean, its wavelength is so long that its rise and fall is practically undetectable. Its speed is about 700km per hour. But when it reaches shallow water, the wave has to slow to about 100km per hour and, as a consequence, piles up into a breaker that surges inland, carrying everything before it and doing untold damage. In the case of the great earthquake in Lisbon, Portugal in 1755, the tsunami, or wall of water, that hit the city shortly after the earthquake, caused more devastation than the earthquake itself.

When Jordan was summoned to Paris to conclude the high profile takeover of Rochelle Eléctronique on behalf of Pilcher Bain, he took the entourage that was his family with him. Joey, aged nine, was on vacation from school; Michelle, at eighteen, was anxious to sign up for a summer course (French Language and Civilization) at the Sorbonne; and I, on leave from the Museum of Fine Arts where I worked as a guide, was all set to take on the role of corporate wife. The fact that we hit one of the hottest summers in living memory, that Jordan's deal ran into eleventh hour problems, that Michelle freaked out on *la vie Parisienne* and Joey missed his pals, was, in view of what happened, immaterial. If an earthquake hits and you are in a secure building, you can strike lucky; confronted with molten lava from an erupting volcano, you can always run; in the face of a tsunami, you don't stand a chance.

Let me tell you something about the Flatlands. Like Mr and Mrs Bun the Bakers and Mr and Mrs Field the Farmers, if you didn't scratch too far below the surface, we were a Happy (enough) Family. Therapy had had its place. Me, early on in our relationship when I had an inexplicable bout of melancholy; Joey, when he fell incomprehensibly behind at school; and Michelle, when she was fighting a losing battle with her adolescent hormones. Three out of the four of us. Not Jordan, to whom the mind was a closed book. With Jordan what you saw was what you got; there was no hassle, no angst. Right was right — his word was his bond, etc. — and you didn't mess with wrong. That was what made him such a good banker. Sometimes, when we were having a discussion about a course of action, something which concerned ourselves or the children, I'd say, but how do you 'feel' about it and he'd say, feelings don't come into it. And they didn't. The psychoanalytic view was that every problem had to have a cause, and that men like Jordan carried a psychological wound brought about by separation from their mothers and their own humiliating inability to give birth or to suckle. It was not that Jordan was deficient in feelings. Just that he wouldn't recognize them if he met them in the street, and after the first few years of marriage, when I grew tired of trying to access them, I accepted him as he was. Which was pretty terrific.

Everyone on Beacon Hill envied us. The Flatlands. We had money — Jordan saw to that; status — he was vice-chairman of the bank; two lovely children; a fine house with a large rear garden and a French country kitchen; Maurice, a handsome Weimeraner (my third child); two hamsters (Joey's); and a posse of friends — 'his', 'hers' and 'ours'. It was a pretty good marriage although unlike some of the couples we knew, Jordan and I were not joined at the hip, which in my book is the recipe for a coma, and we allowed each other plenty of freedom. Life in our circle was pretty good too, despite the fact that children fell sick and loved ones died, and the odd affair left broken marital shards to be picked up and delicately repaired or led to divorce, messy or otherwise, and marauding cancer cells struck indiscriminately, and responded to treatment or did not, drawing those of us who had escaped closer together in communal *Schadenfreude*.

The Flatlands had been lucky. Apart from the usual childhood ailments and Joey's broken collar-bone and Michelle's glandular fever and a couple of basal cell carcinomas on Jordan's back — after which he gave up sitting in the sun — and my own peritonitis from which I almost died, we had escaped pretty lightly. When the call came from Offenbach Frères for Jordan to go to Paris for several weeks to help his corporate manager, Sherman McCurn — Sherman and his wife, Nadine, were our close friends — clinch the Rochelle deal which promised to be a pretty big number, we held a family conclave, the result of which was that the four of us upped sticks and headed for Europe.

It was Lauren who found the apartment in the seventeenth *arrondissement* in the same building as her own, and Pilcher Bain who picked up the tab. Lauren and I had been at school together. Lauren had majored in Modern European Languages and Design while I studied English Literature and Fine Arts, and for three years we had been inseparable. Lauren was a short plump dynamo with a sex problem and it was she who had first abortively dated Jordan while he was still at Harvard; she had lusted after him ever since. It didn't destroy our relationship — mine and Lauren's I mean — for Jordan wasn't the slightest bit interested. Lauren wasn't his type, and the fact that she would have given her right arm to get him into bed was a standing joke. Lauren and I told each other everything — before she landed a serious job as chief designer with a multinational prêt-à-porter fashion house in Paris, and Jordan and I got married, that is. After that it was letters and never-ending telephone calls, then faxes and emails from our respective sides of the Atlantic. It was easier for Lauren. All she had to deal with from me over the years were boring old pregnancies and abortions (one), the usual parental difficulties and run-of-the-mill traumas of marriage and motherhood,

the problems inherent in coping simultaneously with a (part-time) career and family
crises and second homes and one and a half
sets of ageing parents (Jordan had little time
to deal with his mother). Lauren's news, by
contrast, rattled and shook and at times
bordered on the scandalous. Over the years I
had lived with the demands of her demanding
business, her serial affairs, her whistle-stop
tours from Guam to Guyana — 'talk to you
soon, darling' — and the black holes of
depression she fell into from time to time.
When she heard we were coming, *en famille*
to Paris, the text messages flew. She would
find us somewhere to live, pals for Joey,
friends for Michelle, a bolt-hole on the Côte
d'Azur so that we could escape from the
inferno of the city, an au pair to help us and
to babysit Joey so that she and I could go out
on the town. My God, what we weren't only
going to do!

The elegant nineteenth-century apartment,
with its French windows and graceful
wrought iron balcony overlooking the Parc
Monceau, was on the Boulevard Courcelles
where wealthy Parisians lived in stadium-
sized splendour. Mod cons? Forget it. The
apartment was designed neither to impress
nor reassure. The refrigerator was as inadequate, by US standards, as the rooms were

enormous, and both were of similar vintage. When I enquired about en suite bathrooms, Lauren laughed. Despite the appellation, 'en suite' meant little in France. Parisians, many of whom had lived in the same place forever, were conservative where their houses or apartments were concerned, and the clocks of decoration had stopped a long time ago. There were, however, sufficient bedrooms, endless corridors for Joey to race his Red Sox Thunderbird convertible, and several deep and gloomy cupboards for our obscene number of suitcases. The fact that the apartment was on the fifth floor and the caged monolith of an elevator, unreliable, was not reflected in the exorbitant rent. Jordan was not worried about it. He left that side of things to me and I left it to Lauren who could not have been more excited about the prospect of our trip.

As it turned out it was not so much a trip as a cataclysm, no more predictable than the throw of a dice or the spin of a roulette wheel. While a little knowledge of what to do and what not to do when such a dynamic circumstance takes place, together with a little advance planning, can make a big difference to one's chances of survival, I walked into it blind.

2

It was not my first visit to Paris. There had been several trips to Europe over the years and I had spent many happy days gorging myself on the cornucopia of paintings on offer while Jordan wheeled and dealed. We had never visited in August, which at best was not the month of choice and this year managed to produce some of the highest temperatures in living memory. Hot weather and I had never got on and of course there was no such thing as air-conditioning in the Boulevard Courcelles; you could barely open the windows in some of the rooms and it made little difference to the ambient temperature if you did. Parisians didn't worry about such unimportant details. In any case, those who could had left the capital for the mountains, the country, or the Côte d'Azur, fleeing like lemmings, as they did every summer, from the shops with their padlocked doors and handwritten notices proclaiming *fermetures annuelles*, postmen who had gone on strike, and refuse collectors who had come out in sympathy, leaving the overflowing black bags piled up in the streets and stinking rubbish everywhere, not to mention the ubiquitous dog shit.

Most people were bad-tempered and I caught the bug, snapping at Jordan, screaming at Joey, getting confrontational with Michelle (not difficult at any time) and impatient with Helga, the Swiss au pair, a new-comer to domesticity, who had come to help us out and whom I reckoned should be paying me rather than the other way round. Uprooted, before I'd had time to get used to the idea, to prepare myself mentally, I missed my home and I missed what Michelle disparagingly referred to as my 'jobette' at the museum, where I shepherded groups of visitors round the galleries. As we assembled in the foyer I would give them an overview of the building with its dedicated team of curators and museum professionals, for some of whom the special exhibitions — New Egyptian Funerary Arts, Chinese Furniture of the 16th and 17th Centuries, 'Paisley' Motifs from Kashmir to Europe — represented a lifetime of research and study.

My particular area of expertise was the life and work, the one informing the other, of Pablo Picasso. Staking his wits and skill against the world, his images changed with breakneck speed from angst, to radiance and angularity, to voluptuousness with the onset of each new passion. As he transmogrified women into monsters or struck them imperiously from his *oeuvre*, any attempt to analyse the virtuosity with which he seemed effortlessly to bring about the most radical change in painting since the Renaissance, was like trying to nail quicksilver. All I knew was that when I stood before his early Nietzschean notions of creativity — his limpid clowns, his itinerant circus performers, his pictorial expressions of anger and political commitment or his later representations of classical gravity — I was up and away, and far removed from the quiet desperation that governed the mass of most people's lives.

I had little to be desperate about other than the terminal disease that was life itself. On paper I was lady luck personified. A good marriage, no money worries, a more than generous husband, great children, a beautiful home, my health — apart from one or two minor blips — a job and a positive outlook on life. Unlike many of my friends who seemed to live on the brink of a precipice, I accepted who I was, shared my problems, was physically active, learned new skills (I was getting to grips with technology), kept in touch with friends, did something creative (I loved to cook and garden), and was not afraid to ask for help when I needed it. I survived.

Which was more than could be said of many American women in their forties, torn asunder by the conflicting claims of high-powered careers and demanding families, and hopping from one relationship to the next, leaving a trail of forsaken spouses and traumatized children in their wake.

Sometimes, when I was leading my flock through the bewildering array of paintings on offer in the galleries, someone would ask 'how can you tell if a painting is good or not?' followed by the comment that no one would be willing to shell out millions of dollars if *they* were to paint a vase of irises or a bunch of sunflowers. There was no simple answer and the one I was inclined to give was 'luminosity', together with the fact that through the painting the artist had managed to transmit his own feelings. If a work is a 'good' work his emotion will be felt by others and render all interpretations superfluous. If a particular painting does not infect the viewer, no amount of explanation can make it contagious. I did not delude myself that it was a satisfactory response but the truth of the matter was that good art was comprehensible to a great number of people, and if you had to ask the question you would probably be better off in the museum shop among the Chinese calligraphy sets and the art deco card cases and the porcelain ornaments. Don't get me wrong. I did not despise my disciples but you don't become cultured by schlepping round an art gallery. Diverted, yes; entertained, yes; occupied, yes; informed, yes. Not cultured. Not civilized.

Everyone had his reasons. Foreign visitors who came to see what Boston had to offer, and were too busy trying to make a living to frequent the galleries in their countries of origin; veteran tourists, with the Museum of Fine Arts on their whirlwind itineraries, many of whom, preoccupied with bad backs and sore feet took nothing whatsoever away with them apart from a postcard or a poster snapped up on their way to the restroom; philistines who looked more often at their watches than the paintings, and could hardly wait for the moment when it was time for the promised break in the coffee shop. A minority, familiar with the modesty of true art, were extremely knowledgeable. I liked that. I liked engaging in dialogue with those people who loved paintings and who knew what they were talking about. I learned a lot from them and it always made my day as did the schoolchildren, my favourite pupils, gathered round me on their camp-stools and convinced that the haze that enveloped Monet's haystacks was due to the fact that he

16

had been staring at the sun and summer tears were in his eyes.

In one way, Paris and Boston were similar. Both were walking cities. Compact and convenient they could be neatly sliced up into digestible segments like pumpkin pie. The similarities ended there. While Boston was a metropolis with small town sensibilities, Paris was a metropolis: period. Only a hop away from home, Paris, even at the beginning of the twenty-first century, was an aristocrat to Boston's hoi polloi for whom getting and spending had replaced religion, and whose place of worship was the shopping mall — Loulou's Lost and Found with its repro souvenir Maxim's plates and Pan Am ice buckets, or Red Wagon with its funky baby clothes.

Beacon Hill, where we have our house, is Boston's social and geographical pinnacle and the only noise, according to legend, comes from the sound of dust settling on old money. Jordan's family is old money. His mother still lives in a ten-bedroom mansion, with high ceilings and large windows, overlooking Boston Common. A stern woman, who prides herself on the erroneous fact that she hasn't a selfish bone in her body, she demands constant attention and since Jordan's days, weekends often included, are twenty-five hours long, the attending frequently falls to me.

Laetitia Mercy Flatland, strong-minded and with an exalted social position, had managed to produce only one son. I was hardly surprised. One look at the austere body which moved in its own aura, repelling intimacy, and the mind boggled at the notion that she had managed to do anything so down to earth as give birth, not to mention the essential preliminaries. Everything about her, her clothes, her hair in its savage bun, was ascetic, and it was hardly unexpected that her house was furnished in Shaker mode or that her Puritan conscience dictated rigorous self-examination, the acceptance of God's punishment for the smallest sins, a Bible reading to start the day and Church (twice) on Sundays. Had she been born in another era I have no doubt that the mother-in-law that I acquired along with Jordan would not have flinched from spinning wool, dyeing cloth, attending personally to the health of her household and even, when occasion demanded it, performing simple surgery.

Although she lived alone, Laetitia lived in style, dining nightly at a deceptively modest table (it was insured for a small fortune) capable of seating sixteen and which was clean enough to eat from without mats or cloths. There was no such thing as a TV dinner. No such thing as a TV, the emission from which she equated with that from a sewer. She spent her time reading, history mainly — she had a fine mind — making petit point chair seats, cushion covers and bell-pulls that she gave away as Christmas presents — she would have no truck with the garish vulgarity on offer in the shops — listening to opera, Galli-Curci and Rosa Ponselle, and socializing with her equally snobbish friends. Born with a silver spoon in her mouth, she never let you forget it and somehow managed to give the impression that she had not only sprung from some quite other planet but, given the chance, would have taken part with her militant sisters in supporting such historic events as the Boston Tea Party and the Siege of Boston.

She had never quite accepted me. In throwing in his lot with a native New Yorker, Jordan, who was destined for someone much higher up on the social register (I wasn't even on the first rung), had demeaned himself and was constantly reminded by his mother, in subtle and indirect ways, of his seminal gaffe. In my company, looking down upon our friends who were venture capitalists, fund managers and successful professors and doctors, she spoke of heirs to shipping fortunes or industrial entrepreneurs whose financial holdings and far-reaching economic interests assumed a leading role in the affairs of the Bay State. These luminaries wielded extensive political influence, enhanced their dominance through the powerful agency of kinship and marriage, and breathed a rarefied air in which Laetitia made sure I felt deprived of oxygen. When I mentioned to Jordan that I felt ill at ease in his mother's presence he said I was hung up about it and not to take any notice; her bark was worse than her bite. But she didn't bark, that was the trouble; she was much too much of a lady. She hissed like a viper and when she was good and ready and had reduced you to the point where your self-esteem was hovering around nil on a scale of one to ten she went for the jugular, finishing off what remained of you with one sharp thrust of her puritanical tongue.

Once, soon after Jordan and I had become engaged and I sported the family emerald on the fourth finger of my left hand, we were summoned to dinner. The company consisted of a couple of senators and their high-born wives, and a descendant of the Boston Associates, who maintained his pre-eminence in the city by devoting his time and money to supporting cultural, educational and chari-table institutions, one of which was the

Boston Museum of Fine Arts. When the conversation turned to a self-congratulatory exposé of the United States as a bastion of freedom, apparently planted on virgin soil and destined to be a light unto the nations, I blithely ventured an opinion to the effect that this so-called freedom had been built on the sweat of pioneer brows and that, although many Americans had indeed toiled hard, the ultimate source of their prosperity, their start-up capital as it were, lay in what was in reality the theft of a continent and the destruction of those who inhabited it. To say that you could have heard a pin drop would be to put it mildly. The dining-room became distinctly more chill as the senators, steeped in the great American myth and impervious to fact, refused, like most of their fellow countrymen, to contemplate the truth, although deep down they must have known that the wealth and affluence under discussion rested on the shaky foundations of slaughter and slavery. Taking refuge in historical amnesia, Laetitia fixed me with her fading ceanothus-blue eyes and proclaimed in her clipped tones and distinctive nasal twang, 'You are hardly the best judge of the United States, Judith. Your mother, after all, was an *immigrant.*' There were countless other put-downs which I won't go into here, with which she had decimated me over the years. She always seemed to wrong-foot me, no matter how hard I tried, and although I usually managed to wait until I was safely on my way home in the car, I frequently ended up in tears.

There are people like that. Just as some individuals have the knack of making you feel good, others are equally adept at making you feel bad. I only put up with her for Jordan who, incapable of doing wrong — apart from marrying beneath him — was his mother's blue-eyed boy. Funnily enough, Laetitia adored Michelle who didn't have to mind her P's and Q's. Her grandmother's sharp gaze was capable of perceiving only in black or white. While I was black, and nothing I did or could do would alleviate the situation, as far as Laetitia was concerned, Michelle was unequivocally white and could indulge in the most bizarre teenage behaviour without bringing any opprobrium on to her head. She could sit barefoot on the floor fiddling with her toes, play with her long hair which she slung constantly over her shoulder, flaunt her nose stud, guzzle bags of chips in the library, try on her grandmother's rings which she would one day inherit along with her hand-patched quilt and Jordan's oak cradle, and tell the most outrageous stories to do with her love-life which her grandmother never tired of hearing. Perhaps because Michelle was straight up like Jordan — she even looked like him — and wouldn't dissimulate for anyone, she got away with it. Joey was more like me, and Laetitia made no secret of the fact that her monosyllabic grandson, annihilating manic waves of enemy fighters and bombers, or repelling a Mongol invasion on his Game Boy and patiently waiting till it was time to go home, got on her nerves.

We had been in Paris for six blistering weeks and it was one of the hottest of the hot days, when I arrived home with a fretful Joey — who kept dropping the baguettes with which he had been entrusted on to the sidewalk — and enough provisions to sustain a small army, to find that the ailing elevator had finally decided to give up the ghost. The concierge had helpfully attached a note to it, which in a spidery hand on a piece of squared paper torn from an exercise book declared it to be *en panne*. Five floors of steep stairs ahead of us, and the Le Bon Marché bags, some of them laden with frozen food on which I had stocked up, not to mention Michelle's shoe repairs and Jordan's dry-cleaning, weighed a ton.

'What's *en panne*?'

'Broken down. It's not a bit of use rattling the cage.'

Bent almost double, Joey was squinting up the lift shaft, one of the baguettes wobbling perilously.

'I think it's on the fourth floor.'

'It doesn't matter what floor it's on. It's out of order.'

'Why don't they get the repairman?'

'Take this. And this.' I dumped some of the stuff on Joey. 'This is Paris, not Boston.'

'I'm tired, Mom. I'm thirsty . . . ' The baguette fell to the floor.

'Joey!' I didn't mean to scream at him.

'I didn't do it on purpose.'

'Start walking.'

I thumped the button, of which there was one on every landing, to light the first tranche of the broad corkscrew staircase, which proclaimed well-heeled silence and social conformity, its niches filled with plaster busts. Like Joey, I was hot, my Calvin Klein teeshirt was sticking to my back, perspiration was trickling down my legs and I was seriously dehydrated. I stopped for breath on the first half-landing and yearned for Beacon Hill with its serendipity, my house with its mulberry tree and its cool lawn.

It was Michelle's eighteenth birthday and the day had not begun well. Dropping her off at the Sorbonne before taking Joey for his music lesson, I had had an encounter with an HGV followed by an altercation with a van-driver in the Place de la Concorde. Joey was sitting next to me in the Renault with his violin case on his lap, and Michelle, still half asleep — she had been out until the small hours — was in the back fixing her hair and eating a croissant and drinking a *bol* of breakfast coffee when the lorry, which had been tailgating me for some time, drew up alongside. The bronzed driver, wearing a string vest which revealed his muscular torso adorned with tattoos, leaned out of his open window and, kissing his fingertips, smiled down at me provocatively. It was not until I returned his smile with a dazzling one of my own that I realized that the kiss had been directed not at me, but at Michelle. Humiliated, I had neglected to indicate that I was about to take a right turn and had narrowly avoided a collision with a delivery van, the driver of which had treated me to a stream of vernacular abuse which even I, with my limited French, knew had mainly to do with the organs of reproduction.

'Mom!' Joey's voice from the floor below interrupted my thoughts. 'Can I go to Andy's?'

I held the banister and looked down at the

small figure laden with baguettes. Andy was an English boy who lived in the same building.

'After you've done your homework — '

'It's gonna take me two seconds.'

' — and practised the César Franck.'

'Andy's father said we can go swimming.'

'I don't care if the President of the United States says you can go swimming. You have to practise the César Franck.'

It was at that moment, as if to punish me for my lack of generosity, that the lights went out on the staircase leaving us, hung about with heavy shopping and feeling our way, in the dark.

3

I recount all this in detail because later, when my life had been turned on its head, it seemed important to remember the exact sequence of events. After Joey had located the light switch, once more dropping the doomed baguette about which I was too exhausted to comment, we completed the ascent to the fifth floor where in the apartment we found the telephone ringing plaintively and Helga, wielding an impotent mop, standing barefoot in the shallow lake which was the kitchen floor.

'*Der kühlshrank ist kaput.*'

It was the understatement of the year. It hadn't been much of a refrigerator in the first place, but now it and the inadequate freezer compartment that topped it, had finally given up the ghost. By the time I had answered the telephone, which was of course for Michelle, and undergone an inquisition as to her whereabouts and estimated time of arrival, taken the mop from Helga, prevented Joey from scooping up and eating melted and possibly contaminated ice-cream, located the number of a repairman in the *Pages Jaunes* and screamed at him in my execrable French (only partly understanding his voluble response to the effect that the weather was *exceptionel, madame* and his services were at a premium), Joey was in the salon doing battle with the César Franck and Jordan's key was in the door.

Looking at Jordan, his shirt sticking to him, only slightly puffed from the climb — knowing him he would have taken the stairs two at a time — I wondered why he was home so early. Then I remembered with horror that before looking in on Michelle's birthday party, which was to be held at a trendy disco near the Pompidou Center, we were due for cocktails at the Embassy and later on a black-tie dinner, something to do with the bank.

'Hi honey,' Jordan seemed to notice neither my dishevelment nor the fact that I was sporting rubber gloves.

The laboured strains of the César Franck stopped abruptly and erupting from the salon Joey threw himself at his father as the telephone rang again.

'Dad, can I go to Andy's?'

Jordan looked at the telephone then at me. 'Aren't you going to answer it?'

'It'll be for Michelle.'

'Dad, can I . . . ?'

'Sure you can. Why not!'

Glaring at him, I picked up the receiver.

'Hallo? Michelle's out! Sorry. Hang on ... ' I handed the phone to Jordan. 'Sherman.'

'Call him back. I'm going straight into the shower. Fix me a drink, honey. Plenty of ice.'

Had it not been so funny I would have laughed. As it was I stared at Jordan who, having dumped his coat and briefcase, was already on his way to the bedroom peeling off his sodden shirt.

Jordan and I had been married for eighteen years. I was three months pregnant with Michelle when we tied the knot although we pretended to his mother that the baby was premature.

Tall, powerfully built and an all-round athlete with the looks of a movie idol, Jordan Flatland had been every girl's ideal. Intended for politics like his father, he had developed an astonishing aptitude for business and once steered by his Harvard mentors in the direction of banking he had never looked back. Revelling in the world of commerce, in which he was now a star performer, he not only thoroughly enjoyed his work but drew sustenance from it. The fact that he had been made a senior vice-president at Pilcher Bain, a prestigious investment bank, while still in his thirties was due not only to his business acumen, his unique flair for reading the runes of a volatile market-place, but to the fact that he was in addition very much a people person, which was one of the reasons he had come over to clinch the transaction in Paris. An exceptional deal-maker with a deep core of self-assurance, possessed of a unique ability to simplify complex problems and a quiet confidence which concealed his inner drive, he owed his success in pirhana infested waters to the fact that he was a brilliant strategist and that as far as he was concerned all men were equal. He brought out the best in even the worst of them, and made a point of looking not only at his enemies, but at his family and friends with one eye shut. Of course his affable demeanour (he was only rarely ruffled) concealed the streak of ruthlessness, inherited from his mother, that went with the job.

While absolutely determined to succeed, he was not remotely interested in killing the other side. He was the first to acknowledge that there was room on the playing field for everyone and even as his opponents wilted, they regarded Jordan with a grudging admiration. Pleasantly spoken, with no trace of aggression in his voice, he rarely put backs up and had the enviable knack of rejecting and refusing both people and deals with the minimum of offence. Somehow he never turned down anything, be it a suggestion or a sale, outright. Promising to 'think about it' he inspired colleagues with faith, and those who tried to interest him in their wares, with hope. He was possessed of an extraordinary capacity to concentrate on whatever preoccupied him at a given moment, and attracted both men and women by giving them the impression that they filled the whole space of his attention and were a crucial element in some very important enterprise. When Jordan switched off, the light went out and the room went cold.

It was hardly surprising that socially he was much in demand. I was sorry I had not known his father who died when Jordan was fifteen. By all accounts Senator William Flatland, a staunch if misguided Republican, was an equally remarkable man whose marriage to Laetitia was a stable one, if not a union of soul mates. It was not only Lauren — who was desperately looking for a husband — but everyone who knew him who envied me Jordan. Good-natured, considerate and with a happy disposition, he not only *seemed* the ideal husband, but he was. He denied me nothing, be it for myself or the children, tolerated my idiosyncracies, some of which I knew could be maddening, and cheered me up with his unique sense of humour when I was down.

Not that I saw all that much of him. In the cut-throat world of finance, banking was a full-time job. Leaving the house at 6 a.m. — business lunches had long given way to working breakfasts — having already swum several laps of the pool, he was rarely back before 9 at night and if necessary spent evenings and weekends hunched over his laptop or on the phone. Of course there were vacations, but even then, a forward planner par excellence, Jordan did not fully unwind. I never knew if it was because he was indispensable or if he was afraid to let go of the lifeline that was his work. Nevertheless, on holiday he was great company, great fun. We skied as a family, he played baseball on the beach with Joey, and he danced, with more enthusiasm than skill, with Michelle.

Alone at night we would make love — if the earth did not exactly move for either of us, at least it pitched satisfactorily — before he turned over and fell into a well-deserved sleep during the course of which he swore he did not dream. Although our relationship was firmly rooted in affection, friendship, respect for one another and shared values, when it came to mutual interests our paths diverged.

Like any significant pace-setter, Jordan was not well-rounded. He was not really interested in the books I read, did not know what it was to be transformed by an idea, and the most he could manage by way of music or ballet was the *Nutcracker Suite* at Christmas. Although he respected my job, he did not really understand art. Paintings were a commodity — like stocks and bonds — and he regarded the fact that in a thriving market they made fortunes for rich buyers with deeply commercial attitudes as little short of insane. He did read. Usually at night to enable him to wind down. The latest Jack Higgins or Wilbur Smith, turning a few pages only before flinging the paperback on the floor. He was, of course, not uninformed, but his wide knowledge came from the newspapers and financial journals, which he devoured and assimilated, and from late night TV.

As far as Jordan was concerned, the Rochelle Eléctronique deal was crucial and with a bit of luck its successful conclusion would earn him a much coveted seat on the board of Pilcher Bain. One of the functions of the bank was to assist large companies by finding acquisitions for them. Six months ago, Jordan had been approached by Cavendish Holdings, an American semi-conductor manufacturer. The client, whose company last year had made a profit of more than $80 million and whose turnover was rising rapidly, had asked him to find an acquisition which would further their interests in Europe. With the help of various French banks and brokers (Pilcher Bain had first-class contacts), and having produced a shortlist, he had finally come up with Rochelle Eléctronique, a large company which seemed to fulfil the criteria and the appropriation of which he had recommended to the shareholders.

The preliminaries had already been carried out and a couple of the major institutional investors in Rochelle Eléctronique had been to Boston to inspect Cavendish Holdings, the US end of the operation, when Jordan had discovered that by far the biggest shareholder — owning 20 per cent of the company, both directly and indirectly — was the French Ministry of Defence. He had spent the past three weeks in delicate negotiations with Claude Lafarge, a senior civil servant responsible for industrial affairs, in the course of which he had pointed out that the company's sales' margins were improving and its balance sheet was rock solid. All he was waiting for now was for Lafarge to greenlight the proposed merger.

Having divested myself of my rubber

gloves, I followed Jordan into the bedroom with his warm beer and explained about the problems we were having with the fridge. Stripping down to his shorts, he appeared not to hear.

'Guess who took me to lunch at the Crillon today?'

I shook my head. I was still in refrigerator mode.

'Claude Lafarge!'

Sitting down at the dressing-table I looked at my face in the mirror, drained and exhausted. I had overdosed on Claude Lafarge for the past three weeks.

' . . . The MOD has finally agreed the merger!'

Jordan took his beer into the antiquated bathroom across the hallway leaving the door open.

''I like it, Monsieur Flatland . . .'' He gave a passable imitation of Maurice Chevalier. ''*En principe* we are in business. Before I commit myself 'ow-ev-aire' I must discuss with my colleagues. Our people 'ave to go over your people with — 'ow do you say it? — the fine-tooth comb.' It's what we've been waiting for. What have you been up to, honey?'

'Chauffering the kids around . . .'

There were ghastly plumbing noises from

the bathroom as Jordan turned on the shower.

'. . . Vetting Michelle's birthday cake . . . ' My voice was drowned out by ominous rumblings followed by the rush of water.

'Sorry?'

'Vetting Michelle's birthday cake . . . ' I raised my volume, competing with the hiss of steam. ' . . . Entering my trolley for the supermarket Grand Prix, buying underpants for Joey — I don't know what he does with them, waiting for Michelle's shoes to be mended — she needs them for tonight, manning her message desk, listening to Lauren being businesswoman of the year — she sends you a big kiss, picking up the dry-cleaning, helping Helga with her English, sweet-talking the repairman into fixing the freezer *before* we go back to Boston, sanitizing the garbage — the binmen are still out, when I see my waste-disposal I shall probably fling my arms around it, speaking to my mother . . . ' There was silence from the bathroom. I wondered was Jordan still listening. '*Robbing a few cashpoints* . . . ' There was no response. I resumed the liturgy. 'Supervising the César Franck — Joey will not keep his elbow up, taking him swimming, seeing Dr Katz . . . '

She had left Joey at the pool with Andy and

his mother while she kept her appointment with the doctor. It was Jordan who had insisted that she consult him about her headaches. On her last visit to his clinic, after taking a careful history and examining her, Dr Katz had referred her to the path lab where they had taken some blood. Today she had gone to his office for the results of the tests. Suave and thorough, Dr Katz in his white coat had examined her once more, shone lights into her eyes, looked down her throat, palpated her abdomen and listened to her chest with his stethoscope, before leaving her to get dressed while he made up his notes.

'I have found nothing wrong, Madame Flatland,' he said finally, picking up the report from the laboratory. 'Haemaglobin *normale*, thyroid *normale* . . . '

He stared long and hard at her. She wondered if, after all, he had some bad news to impart. Perhaps he suspected a cerebral haemorrhage or a brain tumour which would entail further investigations.

'It's like a tight band . . . ' She indicated the back of her head.

'A little tension, perhaps, in the muscles.'

'I'm pooped out all the time.'

Nodding sympathetically, Dr Katz picked up his pen and drew his prescription pad towards him.

'This formidable heat, Madame. Everyone suffers. Must you remain in Paris?'

Nodding, I muttered something about my husband not being able to get away from the bank, but Dr Katz was not listening.

'Women of your age . . . '

She felt the band round her head tighten. She was forty-two years old. Was he suggesting that she was menopausal? If he was, there was no sign of it. Men. Doctors. They made you sick. She could cheerfully have strangled him. Murder in the Avenue Wagram.

Outside in the street where her car was parked illegally, a traffic warden was waiting for her. She scowled at the woman, chic in her red-trimmed uniform. It was the last straw.

'Did you see Dr Katz?' Jordan, who hadn't been listening to a word, came out of the shower with a towel round his waist.

'He prescribed some medication.'

'Did he say what the headaches are due to?'

'He didn't know,' I lied, refusing to mention the 'm' word.

By the time we were ready for the evening's entertainment — I had tied Jordan's black tie and he had admired my 'blue' Givenchy number, which was actually green; Jordan was colour-blind but would not admit it

— we were both sweating again profusely but the windows with their crimson damask curtains were wide open and the oscillating fan was going flat out and there was nothing we could do about the suffocating heat. Joey was lying on our mahogany *lit-bateau* engrossed in his Pokemon, the all-consuming fascination which baffled everyone over the age of fifteen.

Once I made the mistake of asking him to explain to me exactly what it was he was doing for hours on end, oblivious to everything that was going on around him, and what precisely was a Pokemon. Ask silly questions, you get silly answers. Apparently, there are 150 Pokemons, weird monsters with names such as Jigglypuff and Wigglytuff, possessed with bizarre powers. The idea of the game is that they fight each other, sometimes using twigs as swords, the stronger Pokemon overcoming the weaker. When he wasn't identifying with his other hero, Harry Potter, Joey imagined he was Ash, a streetwise Pokemon trainer, whose mission in life was to collect and subdue all 150 Pokemon monsters, zapping them with his trusty Pokemon ball which drained a Pokemon of his energy.

While he was engaged in battle with Polywig, Polywhirl and Polywrath, I snapped an emerald bracelet round my wrist and secured my hair on top of my head (where I habitually wore it) with a snazzy comb. When Michelle burst in without knocking, Joey did not look up.

One moment I had been perfectly satisfied with my appearance — I thought I looked rather elegant in fact, sophisticated and suitably dressed and filling the corporate wife role to perfection — and the next, as Michelle's image loomed up beside mine in the looking-glass, I wanted to tear the whole lot off and start again. The trend amongst the young was to wear minimal dresses in the flimsiest of material cut on the bias and with spaghetti straps, beneath which Michelle's perfectly rounded breasts sprouted from her armpits. Apart from the apology of a dress and her crazy mane of plum-coloured hair which stuck up in brilliantined spikes and looked as if it had been cut by Edward Scissorhands, but had actually cost an arm and a leg at Biguine, she was naked: no make-up, no jewellery. She looked edible and, despite the Givenchy, the upswept hair and the emerald bracelet, I wondered why I bothered.

She pirouetted, swirling her chiffon skirt in its sweet-pea colours and looking anxiously for reassurance.

'Do you think Félix will like it?'

'You look lovely, darling . . . '

Joey snorted from the bed without taking his eyes from the Pokemon.

'I second that.' Jordan put his arm round Michelle. 'How does it feel to be eighteen?'

Barring the uncertainties and agonizing lack of self-esteem, I would have given my right arm to be eighteen again; to be faced with nothing more taxing than the luxurious prospect of the years ahead and the seemingly endless vista of time begging to be wasted. Having children is the death of parents. Whoever said it did not lie. Seeing them step into your shoes, usurp your spacesuit, take over the asylum, relegate you to a buried memory, a bleached photograph, a residual mass of DNA, accounts for our ambivalent relationship with them, our hostile dependency which leads to rows and misunderstandings that, having been there ourselves, we understand only too well.

Jordan was approaching with a narrow, exquisitely wrapped gift box. The French were so serious about such things, so committed. The most modest purchase, *pour presenter*, in the most isolated village was the cue for assiduous wrapping complete with spiral bow.

'Happy birthday, darling.' He gave the package to Michelle.

''Happy birthday, darling.'' Without raising his eyes from the Pokemon, Joey mimicked Jordan as Michelle took off the ribbon and the paper and opened the Bulgari box.

The pearls were exquisite. Although I had chosen them (Jordan was too busy), Jordan had insisted on giving them to her, it had to do with his *amour propre* and the fact that it was his money that had paid for them, as if Michelle did not know.

'I don't deserve them.'

'You can say that again.'

'Shut up, Joey.'

'Who said anything about deserving them?' Jordan fastened the necklace around the untrammeled skin of Michelle's throat. She looked virginal although I knew that she was not. With tears in her eyes she hugged us both like an affectionate puppy. At the same moment the roar of a motor-bike accompanied by a staccato signal on the horn came from the street below. Casting us off without more ado, Michelle stuck her head out of the open window.

'*J'arrive!*' It was the voice of a fishwife.

She kissed me briefly.

'See you guys . . . ' She flung her arms round Jordan, mussing his hair. 'Gotta go.'

Minutes later, leaning out of the window, I watched her run out of the building to greet the black-clad motorcyclist who sat astride a Kawasaki 2000. She must have flown down the stairs. They kissed three times, formally, alternating cheeks. Michelle climbed on to the pillion, held on to the young man's waist and with a roar they were away, weaving amongst the rows of parked cars and leaving behind a trail of vapour and the diminishing cacophony of strident rap.

Jordan was dictating a message to his PA into his memo machine. 'Eunice, I want you to find out if there's been any heavy buying . . . ' He looked impatiently at his Rolex, before turning to me. 'Are you ready, honey? I don't want to be late.'

4

The cocktails at the American Embassy restored my equilibrium. Jordan and the current ambassador, whose wife was Swedish, had been at Harvard together. It was mega-hot and mega-crowded but I could see from the appraising glances of the women — no slouches when it came to putting themselves together — and the roving eyes of the men, that the Givenchy was going down well. So much for Dr Katz.

The French of course were into protocol. My hand was sore from being shaken and my head dizzy from introductions to people whose names I was unable to retain for more than a nanosecond, amongst whom were several senior French bankers who presented us to other bankers of various denominations.

''Monsieur Jordan Flatland, senior vice-president of Pilcher Bain. Madame Flatland.'' I allowed the tips of my fingers to be kissed as I looked into a pair of predatory eyes that might once have been enticing but were now milky with cataracts.

'*Enchantée.*' I switched on my corporate smile.

''Monsieur Jordan Flatland, senior vice-president of Pilcher Bain, Madame Flatland . . . ''

'I knew your father-in-law, my dear. The Porcellian Club . . . '

'Flatland?' The accent was from the American deep south. 'Jordan Flatland? Haven't I been reading about you in the newspaper?'

'Pilcher Bain,' Jordan was flattered. 'Our client Cavendish Holdings is making a bid for Rochelle Eléctronique.'

Clutching our champagne flutes, we managed to make our way to the familiar faces in the Pilcher Bain corner: Sherman McCurn, Jordan's corporate manager, and his wife, Nadine. Sherman, a great communicator, was the ideal partner to disseminate Jordan's strategic wisdom. The two men not only complemented each other in business but played regular squash together, and he and Nadine and Jordan and I had dinner together at one of Boston's eateries at least once a week. When there were no social engagements or we were too lazy to go out, usually on the weekend, we'd play Scrabble for money or watch a movie over a pizza.

I greeted the Shermans as all eyes swivelled to a stooped and elderly financier who stood framed in the doorway looking up with adoration at a vapid-looking blonde, wearing short shiny satin and dangly diamond earrings, who was draped over his arm.

Nadine's eyes nearly popped out of her head. 'Where did Stanley find her?'

'He opened his wallet and there she was.' Sherman kissed me on both cheeks as snatches of conversation floated in bubbles around our heads.

' . . . As I read it they're looking to develop a diversified portfolio of franchises . . . '

' . . . I said it's not a bit of use you coming over in August. Paris is a morgue . . . '

' . . . is it true the Japanese are moving in . . . ?'

' . . . Cultural Attaché! If you want my opinion he should be in Macy's selling kitchen appliances . . . '

'Boston? I just adore Boston. American body and European soul.'

' . . . 'Dad, the Bank of America will lend me a million dollars if you will guarantee it.' 'Son,' the father says, 'go tell the Bank of America that *I* will lend you a million dollars if they will guarantee it . . . ''

'Hi Jordan!' Eric Boone, Bank of Nova Scotia, edged his way through the heaving crowd towards us, clutching several glasses and inadvertently spilling champagne on to Jordan's sleeve.

'Excuse me. I'm so sorry . . . '

Trying not to show his annoyance — a stain on his clothes was like a stain on his life — Jordan took out his handkerchief and dabbed melodramatically at the damp patch on the tux I had just collected from the dry-cleaner.

' . . . Any news on the acquisition front?'

Regaining his composure, Jordan put away the handkerchief and, crossing his fingers, addressed Boone.

'As of today I think we're in business.'

'The smart money's on you, Flatland.'

Jordan's face lit up with delight as the Canadian banker turned to me. 'They'll be making this young man president of the Central Reserve Bank next!' Chuckling, he moved on with his slopping glasses.

Sherman, cautious at the best of times — he was the counterbalance to Jordan's perpetual optimism — took Jordan to one side.

'I'm still a bit uneasy about Lafarge. What if he's only the mouthpiece? The ministry's front man.'

Jordan plucked a glass from the silver tray held by a waiter wearing white gloves. Nothing could prick the balloon of elation engendered by his lunch with the man from the ministry.

'Claude Lafarge is eating out of my hand. I guarantee we'll be back in Boston in time to see the Red Sox play Oakland.'

'What I'd like to know is who *he* has to report to.'

'I hope to God it's all over . . . ' Nadine, in a little white suit, was fanning herself with her little white purse.

'Jordan thinks so.' I had every faith in Jordan.

'What I wouldn't give for my pool . . . '

'Monsieur, *s'il vous plaît.*'

There was a flash as a photographer separated Jordan from Sherman and took his picture. On instruction, Jordan put his arm around me and we posed together for *Vanity Fair*. '*M. et Madame Jordan Flatland à l'Ambassade Américaine.*'

Dinner was in the Avenue Foch at the home of the Minister of Trade and went on for ever. Aubergine with crab was followed by *médaillons de boeuf* which gave rise to a discussion about Creutzfeld-Jacob Disease and the perils of English beef, and was followed by Timbale Orta — an unsuitably hot cherry pudding with a sabayon sauce — which most of the women refused. I was trapped between a tedious agronomist and an *éxpert-comptable*, whose English was decidedly worse than my French, and as soon as the coffee had been served I tried to catch the eye of Jordan who was being his customary affable self to an inebriated fifty-year-old with a corrugated cleavage.

It was well after midnight by the time the limo, put at our disposal by Offenbach Frères, dropped us at Les Bains. Blinded by the strobe lights and deafened by the noise, which must have been close to causing nerve damage, we hacked our way — me in my Givenchy and Jordan in his black tie — through the jungle of gyrating bodies and entwined couples of various gender combinations, in search of Michelle.

She was at a table piled high with wrapping-paper and presents, scented candles, chocolates and flowers, surrounded by the friends she had accumulated during our short stay in Paris.

'Hi, Mom! Hi, Dad! Guys, this is my mom and dad,' she shrieked. 'Félix — '

I recognized the young man with the Kawasaki who was deep in conversation with his moustachioed companion.

' — and his *copain*, Alexandre. Alexandre is my history tutor . . . '

'Was!'

I remembered it was the last day of her course.

'Anything you want to know about Napoleon . . . '

''Napoléon Bonaparte . . . '' the chant from the assembled gathering came over the music. ''Général at 24, First Consul at 30, Emperor at 34, exiled at 45, dead at 51. The most fascinating 'uman being in 'istory . . . ''

'Press the right button, Alexandre will tell you the story of Napoléon's wallpaper.'

'Okay you guys,' Michelle continued with the introductions as they fell about laughing. 'Nicolas, Laurent, Natasha, Frédéric, Kiki — Lois you know — Juliette . . . '

A joint was being passed around. Some of them looked half asleep. One of the boys liberated more chairs and Félix stood up attentively, making more space so that I could sit down beside him. There was champagne on the table, courtesy of Jordan, and the birthday cake I had ordered from Fauchon with its eighteen pink candles. Félix filled my glass. Dressed in black and in his late twenties, his face dark with stubble beneath luxuriant black hair, he looked older than the rest.

'I'm Michelle's mother,' I said superfluously. Looking round the table I felt like her grandmother, trussed, like a chicken, in my shimmering green dress.

'Félix Dumoulin,' he held out his hand. 'You could be her sister.' His eyes were serious.

'You speak very good English.'

'I studied in London. One year at the Slade. Afterwards the École des Beaux Arts.'

'You're an artist?'

'I paint.'

'Félix is brilliant,' Michelle shouted. 'He's had a whole bunch of exhibitions. He won't tell you himself.' Gazing at him with adoration she picked up the matches to light the candles on her birthday cake and I wondered how involved she was and if she was sleeping with him or if, on the other hand, Félix and Alexandre . . .

''Happy Birthday to you.'' It was Jordan, flanked by two of Michelle's girlfriends, juicy as ripe peaches and patently hitting on him, who started the singing. The chorus was taken up first by the table and later by the band, augmented by the enthusiastic voices of everyone in the room, who neither knew who Michelle was nor cared, and carried on dancing or snogging or whatever it was they were doing. More champagne was poured and Michelle, her face flushed and her pupils dilated, raised her glass.

'Thank you all for coming to my party,' her voice was hoarse. 'And thank you for your wonderful presents . . . '

Going round the table she embraced everyone in turn. When she came to Félix, she kissed him long and hard on the mouth to the accompaniment of slow handclaps and catcalls. I already had them walking down the aisle before I remembered this was the twenty-first century and got a grip on myself.

When order was restored and Michelle had resumed her seat, she indicated the cake with its eighteen flickering candles and the unseemly number of empty champagne bottles — Jordan never did things by halves — and put a hand to the pearls around her neck.

'I'd like to thank my parents — quiet everybody — for everything . . . and . . . for-putting-up-with-me-for-eighteen-years!'

This time they fell about laughing. The girls, like so many floral moths with white faces and scarlet lips, were crying melodramatically on each other's necks and kissing one another and getting up to hug Michelle who with fat tears rolling down her face was attempting to blow out the joke candles (Joey's idea) which sprang to life again each time they were extinguished.

When the flames had died away from all but one of them, I leaned across the table — typical mother — and reached out to extinguish the flame. As it scorched my fingers I recoiled in pain and Félix, who was the only one to have noticed, reached for my hand and turned over my palm to ascertain the extent of the damage. Our eyes locked for the briefest of moments, activating a network I'd thought dormant in my brain. The glance which passed between us was gone so quickly I thought that I must have imagined it, and that the music and the champagne — on top of all the wine I had imbibed earlier — must have gone to my head.

To cover my confusion I got up and prised a reluctant Jordan from between his two admirers, snapping my fingers in time to the Salsa and pulling him to his feet. Michelle looked mortified, and once we had staked our claim to a few square inches of available space amongst the flailing arms and scantily dressed bodies, I understood why. Given the eighty-seven years we clocked up between us and Jordan's lack of co-ordination on the dance floor, we were well past our sell-by date as far as the Salsa was concerned. It was Michelle who prevented us from making complete fools of ourselves. Jumping up and down, like a little rubber ball, with Félix who towered heavily above her, she grabbed Jordan's arm and yelled, 'You're supposed to dance with the birthday girl!' and we changed partners in the middle of the heaving, thumping floor.

Making no attempt to dance with me, a

decision which at the time I made no effort to interpret, Félix led the way back to the table, holding my chair, with a maturity which belied his years, until I was seated.

'*Superbe!*'

'I'm sorry?'

'The dress.' He was admiring the Givenchy.

'Thank you.' I raised my voice above the music.

'*Jade . . .* ' The 'j' was soft. '*Comme vos yeux.*'

When novelists mention eyes, the colour usually has banal implications: blue, innocence and honesty; black, passion and depth; and brown, reliability and common-sense. Flaubert, on one page gives Emma Bovary brown eyes, on another deep black eyes, and on yet another, blue.

'You've read *Madame Bovary?*'

Startled out of my wits, I wondered had I been thinking aloud and was about to ask him when we were interrupted by Jordan who had left the dance floor and was looking anxiously at his Rolex.

I turned to Félix. 'We have to go. My husband has a busy day tomorrow.'

We embraced Michelle who thanked us for the party all over again, said goodbye to her friends, and weaved our way through the cauldron of bodies to the door.

In the back of the limo, I was again conscious of the tight band round my head as I reran the events of the night. We were glad to get home until we saw that the elevator was still *en panne* — I don't know what we had expected — and there were no cold drinks in the fridge.

Sitting on the carved stool in the bedroom, I kicked off my shoes and massaged my aching feet. Jordan was examining the sticky patch on his sleeve where the champagne had been spilled.

'I'll leave it here.'

Confident that like a good little Stepford wife I would once more ferry his tux to the dry-cleaner, he arranged the midnight-blue jacket carefully over the back of a chair before going across the hallway to the bathroom to clean his teeth.

'Who was the young man?'

'Which young man?' I made an attempt to sound casual.

'Michelle's . . . ' Sounds of swishing and spitting. Jordan was an obsessional teeth cleaner. 'The black hairy one. What was his name?'

'Félix.'

'We may have to keep an eye on him.'

'Don't worry about it . . . ' Relieved of my shoes, slipping out of my dress and waving my arms above my head, I salsaed round the *lit-bateau* free of the restraints of the Givenchy. 'Michelle's going away soon.'

'What *are* you doing, honey?' I hadn't heard Jordan come in. He looked at me in amusement. 'Aren't you tired?'

Strangely enough I was not, and by the time I was ready for bed I felt an urgent desire to make love but, although it was two-fifteen and Jordan had to be up in a few hours, he was working away on his laptop.

5

The lugubrious repairman who wore pristine white overalls, had dismantled the refrigerator and distributed its components all over the kitchen floor, Joey was attending to his tropical fish — cleaning out the tank with a messily leaking hose attached to the tap, Helga was painstakingly ironing a many ruffled blouse in preparation for a party, and I was snatching a quick cup of coffee before going to meet Lauren for our weekly Pilates session at Le Studio, when Jordan called from Offenbach Fréres to say that he had invited Monsieur and Madame Lafarge for dinner.

'Tell Jordan . . . nobody in Paris . . . entertains at home.' Pursing her lips, Lauren exhaled noisily as, squeezing a rubber ball between her ankles, she slid back and forth purposefully on the *plié* machine in the interests of her inner thighs.

'I *tried* to tell him . . . ' Lying on the exercise bed next to her, I manoeuvred a one-and-a-half-kilo weight slowly over my head. 'I called him straight back when it had sunk in. Spoke to his PA. 'In a meeting. All day.''

Eunice had been sympathetic. A woman of a certain age, she had been Jordan's right hand for many years and was deeply in love with him. Accepting, pragmatically, that her devotion for her employer was unrequited and always would be, she took a vicarious interest in his family, involving herself in his domestic life.

'It's August. He probably thought that most of the best restaurants would be closed . . . ' Lauren sprang immediately to Jordan's defence.

'He didn't *think*!'

'You like to cook . . . '

It was true. Although by inclination a feminist, I was at the same time a dinner-on-the-table wife. The dichotomy was one of my problems.

'At home! With my own *batterie de cuisine* . . . '

Lauren had no idea what I was talking about.

'Fauchon do a Vichysoisse to die for . . . '

I told her about the fridge, the bottom line of which was that it needed a new condenser, and that the factory was closed and it looked as if it was going to be out of action for some time. Warm Vichysoisse was a definite non-starter (if you'll excuse the pun), particularly if Jordan was hoping to impress the Lafarges. Lauren wasn't listening; still working her legs, she was speaking to one of her suppliers on her mobile, which was strictly forbidden in the health club.

'*Oui! Oui! J'écoute.*' She sounded angry. '*Numéro 3240. Marron foncé. Foncé. Non . . . Je ne peux pas le croire!* Brown. Dark brown. I faxed it to you on . . . Sorry, I don't have my briefcase right here. *Numéro 3240*. I'll call you back! That's all I need after last night . . .' I realized she was addressing me and remembered that she had been out with a new date.

'Boring, boring, boring. Three hours in Castel banging on about his ex-wife. You can keep your Latin lovers. Eat too much. Smoke too much. And keep their socks on in bed! Give me a Harvard man any day of the week. You don't know how lucky you are, Judith.' She returned to her telephone. '*Veuillez me passer Madame Clothilde, s'il vous plaît, de la part de Madame Robinson* . . . '*Le monde de la mode!*'' She gesticulated with the phone. 'It's still summer, Judith. 'Think light: think linen.' And here am I kicking ass for mohair mufflers and puffy jackets . . . *Allo?* Madame Clothilde?'

By the time she had finished shouting at everyone, Lauren had used up so much energy that we decided to call it a day. When we came out of the showers, a young girl, slim as a reed, was towelling her hair. Lauren, who was five-foot nothing and fought an ongoing battle with her weight, confronted her body in the uncompromising mirror.

'Inside every fat woman is ... a fat woman.' She removed her locker key from her wrist.

Outside Le Studio we went our separate ways. Lauren to her office, me to the dry-cleaner for the second time in two days.

Lauren kissed me on both cheeks then gave me an extra one for Jordan.

'*Bonne chance* for tonight.'

I watched her bustle into the distance with her Louis Vuitton briefcase before I went to find my yellow Renault which I had parked in the rue du Temple and which was like a sauna. Preoccupied with my irritation at Jordan's cavalier behaviour and the hundred and one menus which were fast-forwarding through my head, it was not until I had fastened my seat belt, turned on the ignition and grasped the molten steering-wheel that I noticed the red rose on my windscreen. I presumed it had been dropped in the gutter from which a passer-by had retrieved it and tucked it beneath the wiper.

In the end I settled on an hors d'oeuvre of the finest smoked salmon, with which you could never go wrong, and *Poulet de Bresse* roasted with brandy and tarragon. Fortunately the French were not into puddings and I reckoned that a Chaumière, served on the house cheese plates which bore the legend *Bleu d'Auvergne, Fromage de Chèvre Doux* and *Coeur de Neufchâtel*, followed by a bowl of rosy-hued apricots, would go down well.

From the moment they'd arrived, Lafarge, formal, in a formal suit in which he must have been sweltering (particularly after his climb up the stairs), and elegant Madame, fresh from the coiffeuse and bearing heliotropes, decked out in taupe *peau de soie* garnished with glittery buttons, I'd known that not only were we in for a long and serious haul, but that the success of the evening was of paramount importance to Jordan.

Despite the heat and the fact that I had been slaving over a hot and antiquated stove in my tip of a kitchen, the dinner itself went more smoothly than the conversation which, impeded by Madame Lafarge's lack of English and only slightly helped by the Château Cos d'Estournel that Jordan opened, never really got off the ground. Dragging a reluctant Joey away from Polywig and Polywhirl, I used him as an ice-breaker but the Lafarges, who apparently had none of their own, whether by accident or design, were not particularly interested in children. While Madame — I never did discover her first name — nodded distantly at the sight of a small boy, a Jordan clone in striped pyjamas, Lafarge enquired with as much gravitas as if he were addressing an ambassador, what Joey missed most about leaving Boston. The reply, 'strawberry-mousse-cup-from-Bildeners-and-pancakes-with-maple-syrup', gave rise to an attempt at translation for the benefit of Madame Lafarge who smiled with more enthusiasm than comprehension. After dinner, Jordan got down to business with Lafarge over balloons of his finest brandy, leaving me to slog it out with Madame, face to face on the unyielding sofas in the uncomfortable salon.

It was as if the evening had been choreographed by French protocol with Jordan as the conductor and myself as the *metteur en scène*. Even with the doors on to the balcony wide open, the temperature, which was still in the eighties with not a trace of a breeze, was not on my side. Juggling my roles of chief cook and bottle-washer, master of ceremonies and waitress — Jordan could not leave the table — I had done my best with Lafarge, who was decidedly challenged in the small-talk department. Engaging him in conversation was like wading through treacle, and I'd waited patiently while he decoded my every remark for the benefit of an increasingly moist-faced Madame.

By the time they were ready to leave I was a gibbering idiot and convinced that I had clobbered Jordan's chances, as far as Rochelle Eléctronique was concerned, with the Ministry of Defence. When the kissing and the hand-shaking formalities were completed and Jordan had accompanied the Lafarges to the street so that he could attend to the lights on the stairs, I closed the door firmly on the battlefield that was the dining-room, flung myself wearily on the bed and waited for the inevitable post-mortem.

'Lafarge thought you were *formidable*!' Jordan, who in the interests of decorum had had to keep his jacket on all through dinner, could not wait to strip off. 'I thought you were pretty *formidable* myself. You did a great job. You know how much Rochelle Eléctronique means to me.'

I had had Rochelle Eléctronique morning, noon and night for the past six months. I could not tell Jordan but, combined with the weather and the inconveniences of Paris, I was *ras le bol* with Rochelle Eléctronique and would be glad when it was all over.

I couldn't believe that after all the traumas

of the evening he still had the stamina to make love. That was Jordan. He had boundless energy. It went with the job. Eviscerated by the events of the day — it seemed a lifetime ago since the repairman had done battle with the fridge — the only thing I wanted to do was to crawl into bed, or rather to lie on top of it, and sleep. Knowing that to refuse Jordan, who was hovering expectantly, in his present fraught state, would be to knock a nail in the coffin of Rochelle Eléctronique, I held out my arms as the telephone rang and he answered it. I knew it could only be Sherman.

He stroked me absent-mindedly with one hand as he filled his partner in with the events of the evening.

' . . . It went good. Judith excelled herself . . . ' He kissed my neck. 'I think you can put Leroy and his team on standby. Why don't you call them? My guess is that they should get their asses over here by the end of next week. We'll have to take a look at the fiscal situation and liaise with the tax people over here. We don't want to land ourselves with hefty bills . . . '

Saying goodnight to Sherman and reassuring him that his call hadn't woken us, Jordan turned once more to me, this time giving me his full attention.

'Sorry about that, darling.'

When you have been married as long as Jordan and I have, making love can be a bit of a minefield. Given the nature not only of our genes but the various demands of our working days, it could at times be like going up the down escalator. When Meg Ryan faked an orgasm in a crowded restaurant in the seminal scene of the hit movie *When Harry Met Sally*, there was not a woman in the audience who did not empathize with what was going on. Women are born to fabricate and men are easy to deceive. It is the way of the world.

Watching the Venetian chandelier — which needed a good clean — above my head, I did my best to join in the fun while my brain took off in a multitude of directions to do with Michelle and the fact that she was going away, and whether the chicken could have done with another fifteen minutes and if the Lafarges had noticed, and the burden of shopping every single day until the refrigerator was fixed, and wondering what time Helga would turn up after her party and whether I was responsible for her welfare, and should I have worn tights like Madame Lafarge instead of prancing around bare-legged . . .

'Sorry?'

Already Jordan, invariably considerate, was asking how was it for me. 'Great,' I said. 'It was fine.'

With hindsight tights would have been a good idea, but how was I to know?

In the morning Jordan brought me coffee in bed before he went to the bank. 'Thank you for last night. The Lafarges were impressed.'

He was a good and considerate man. He had enough on his mind at the moment. Sometimes I thought I didn't appreciate him enough. I got married to Jordan when I was very young. He was one of my first boy-friends. Today we would probably have lived together — in Michelle's eyes marriage conjured up images of boredom and dullness; every film, every song was about dangerous liaisons and where was the *frisson* in marriage? But I'm still not at all convinced that it's such a good idea. I'm not the kind of person that does a trial anything. Being tested makes me nervous.

I wanted to tell Jordan that inviting the Lafarges home had probably been a good move on his part, they at least seemed to have enjoyed the evening, but he had switched on his memo-machine and was walking round the room as he dictated into it.

'Memo to Judd Barnard, Boston, re.

Rochelle Eléctronique. The tax boys here have advised two tax havens. Investment income through one and exports through the other. I'd appreciate your views on this. Say goodbye to Michelle . . . '

It was today that Michelle was going away.

' . . . I'll try to call her from the office.'

Stuffing the memo-machine into his pocket, he ruffled my hair, kissed my forehead — I could smell the shower soap — and was gone, bedecked with his coat, his briefcase, his laptop and his mobile phones. I thought he looked very sexy but of course Jordan had other things, not the least of which was Rochelle Eléctronique, on his mind.

By the time I got up, Helga, still in her frilled blouse, mascara careering down her face, was sitting at the kitchen table over a tisane, reading a letter from Germany. There was no sign of Michelle.

'How was the party?'

'It was good.' She yawned ostentatiously.

I wondered if Hans-Dieter, whose ring she wore on her finger, would appreciate the fact that his betrothed had stayed out all night and was probably up to no good. I indicated the fallout from the previous night's cooking. 'I'm afraid there's rather a mess . . . '

Helga looked at me blankly. Giving the

encrusted roasting-tin and the pots and pans in the sink up as a bad job, I made breakfast for Joey, who was absorbed in the Black Mollys and Dwarf Gouramis that rose pouting to the surface as he dropped in their morning flakes, and went to wake Michelle.

With her thumb in her mouth, a habit she had not grown out of, and covered only by a sheet — her narrow room looked out on to a well and was already unbearably hot — she was in the foetal position, sleeping like a baby. About to lose her, if only for a few weeks, I allowed myself to remember the night she was born. Jordan had been hoping for a boy. It doesn't matter what major events happen to you in life, there is still nothing to touch the birth of a child, particularly your first. Although today having a baby is, by and large, a joyful, privileged experience compared with the suffering and loss of maternal and infant life of a hundred years ago, nothing can prepare you for the earth-shattering pain, the unbelievable pleasure — the impression of being at one with the world, the post-orgasmic sensation, the tingling in every fibre of your being — of delivering a nine-pound bundle, which physiologically is far too large for the birth canal. Arriving, as she did, late (a habit she was not to relinquish) and unexpectedly and before there was time either for the niceties of the waterbirth for which I had elected or an epidural, Jordan and I only just made it to the hospital, before Michelle, crying vigorously, made her appearance on the stage and changed the face of our world.

With Joey it was different. Firstly I had had an amniocentesis at sixteen weeks, so the fact that the baby turned out to be a boy was no surprise, and secondly because of difficulties with the presentation — spine to spine, which once would have led to abandonment to my fate — he was born by Caesarian section. Whether it was because he was my second child and I, a seasoned mother, or that I was preoccupied with the abdominal scar and severed muscles which were consequent upon his birth and caused considerable discomfort, I don't know. The two experiences could not be compared. It might of course have been the fact that every mother contains her daughter in herself and every daughter her mother, and that every woman extends backwards into her mother and forwards into her daughter, a phenomenon which gives rise to sensations of immortality. Michelle and I were part of a feminine conspiracy and despite our differences, despite the hostility, jealousy, and sniping endemic between mothers and daughters — she got on a great deal better with Jordan with whom she forged an opposition alliance — we were somehow inextricably bonded. Like most mothers I yearned to put my hard-earned experience at the disposal of her young life, but I knew that she had to enter the lists for herself.

She was so soundly asleep that I was reluctant to wake her. I touched her face, envying her her flawless skin and aware that mine, despite the latest anti-ageing creams, was already beginning to lose some of its elasticity. She was smiling in her sleep and it seemed a pity to disturb her. I put my hand on her shoulder.

'Time to wake up. Lois will be here soon.'

Lois was from Los Angeles where her father produced movies. Michelle had met her on the Sorbonne course and they were to travel together. When there was no response and the steady pattern of Michelle's breathing did not change, I looked round the room at the discarded underwear and half-worn teeshirts, the shorts and sneakers and diaphanous skirts which lay like sighs on the floor ready to go into the flaccid rucksack. The flags of her freedom.

6

The two girls, wearing shorts and tank-tops, stood in the hall on the threshold of their lives while I, knowing that I was doing it and hating myself for it, fussed round like a mother hen wittering on about tickets and passports and money-belts and credit cards and remembering to email frequently with their whereabouts. Far from being embarrassed at my behaviour — you'd think they were venturing into outer space instead of wandering around Europe and ending up with friends of Lois's in Tuscany — Michelle who was used to it, did not even notice. She was too busy shouting at Joey who in attempting to lift the open rucksack on to his narrow back while she put a last minute lace in her hiking boots, had disgorged some of the contents, including a copy of *The Hitchhiker's Guide to the Galaxy*, maps, flip-flops and a box of Tampax, on to the floor. Among the detritus I recognized my Calvin Klein teeshirt.

Michelle's eyes met mine as she stuffed it into the rucksack. 'Okay, okay . . . I swear I'll bring it back.'

'Are you going to bring me a present?' Joey, who had even abandoned his Pokemon in order to see his sister off, sounded wistful. Despite the age difference, which had not been deliberate but was the way things had worked out, he was going to miss her.

'If you stop being a pest.'

'Michelle!' Sensing an injustice, I defended Joey's corner.

'Okay, *okay*!' Fastening the rucksack, Michelle addressed me. 'I left my Levis on the bed. The zipper's jammed.'

Decoding this message as 'take my jeans to the alteration shop and get them fixed by the time I come back', I bit my long-suffering mother's tongue, both in the interests of a harmonious parting and the fact that Lois was there. Together with Helga, apparently now recovered from her *nuit blanche* and with a towel round her hair, which predicated another hour blow-drying her crowning glory while the dishes remained in the sink, I managed to hoist the rucksack up on to Michelle's tanned shoulders, wondering how the two girls could possibly stagger to the métro never mind make their way round Europe.

Michelle flung her plump arms around me. From the warmth of the embrace I knew that I wasn't the only one who was a little bit afraid.

'Bye, Mom. Say hi to Daddy for me. I called the office . . . You have to make an appointment to speak to him these days.'

'He said to say goodbye. Take care . . . '

' ''Don't do anything I wouldn't do.'' Joey's voice was a passable imitation of my own.

I kissed Lois on both cheeks.

'Cheers Mrs Flatland.'

'Look after each other.'

Opening the front door for them, as if they could not even manage that, I pressed the bell on the elevator.

'Mom!' Joey rolled his eyes to the ornate ceiling.

I had forgotten they would have to yomp down five flights of stairs.

When they had gone the apartment felt empty. As if the life had gone out of it; which it had. Little as Michelle's chaotic lifestyle fitted with our own, I missed her already and wanted to run after her with help and advice, to keep her, not only safe but grappled to my side. We had had the promiscuity and sex talks when Michelle was twelve, although even at that tender age it was spitting in the wind. The drugs spiel came later when I had been shocked to hear that many of the kids, some of them well-educated teenagers who had been indoctrinated with the myth of 'responsible drug-taking' and 'harm-free' drugs, were passing on the hash and going straight for the hard stuff. As parents it bothered us that the substances were so easily available. Both Jordan and I had tried to impress upon Michelle that cannabis — even one joint smoked every other day — hung around in the blood for weeks, hit the immune system, inhibited performance, could result in permanent brain damage, and that drug-dealing was the most corrupt industry in modern society.

Watching Michelle and Lois venture into the unknown equipped only with their backpacks, into which their lives had been summarily crammed, I knew that I was a little bit jealous. When Jordan and I travelled, which we did quite frequently, it was never economy and usually five star hotels; Jordan would no longer have any truck with the romantic hideaways of our early marriage with their sagging beds, non-existent service and lack of business facilities. Going away meant mental lists of what to take (if not actually packing) at least three weeks in advance, itemized plans concerning Joey's schedule of extra-curricular activities and social life, and stocking the freezer and planning for emergencies to lighten the load on my mother who flew in from Florida to look after him. It seemed a lifetime back that

I had light-heartedly headed for the Adirondacks (India had been a no-no as far as my mother, who feared dirt and disease, was concerned), a long time since I could simply get up and go.

The day stretched before me, empty and vapid. I would tidy Michelle's room so that Helga could clean it, take her Levis to be mended, touch base with Nadine, drop Joey at his violin lesson on the Left Bank and, while I was waiting for him, do my shopping in the rue de Buci. Enervated by the heat, although it was not yet midday, and not yet ready to face my chores, I flopped on the bed and dialled Nadine's number.

The three of us, Lauren, Nadine, and myself, had been at high school together although Nadine, who had had an abortion which had gone sadly wrong resulting in a hysterectomy at the age of eighteen, had dropped out and entered finishing school in Switzerland where the acquisition of fluent French and German — she was a natural linguist — had been no disadvantage. Of Catholic origin and the oldest of four brothers and three sisters, she had put her organizing abilities to good use and as CEO of *Anyoccasion.com* was Boston's number one party planner. Much in demand when there was a birthday or wedding to be celebrated, an art gallery to be subsidized, a theatre to be funded, a charity to be launched or a benefit to be shored up, she could put together anything from a mini-makeover for precocious nine-year-olds to a full-scale reproduction of the Palace of Versailles complete with Marie-Antoinette ball gowns, waiters dressed as flunkeys, imported Alpine and Japanese gardens and fountains which spurted champagne.

Once she had invited Jordan and me to a black-tie dinner (5,000 dollars a plate to refurbish the Opera House), which embodied the cream of Boston new money. Aware of the fashionistas I would be up against, I had opted for a chic black dress and had had my hair styled and my nails freshly manicured to show off my Flatland engagement ring. I thought I had done a good job, but no sooner had I entered the arena of the Four Seasons Hotel than I felt like Little Orphan Annie. At our table alone, among the svelte bodies — their delicate systems sustained by egg-white omelettes, organic carrot petals and wheat-free everything — there was a gown of chrome sequins topped with a head-hugging helmet of yellow turkey feathers, a white leather mink-trimmed two-piece which revealed a taut midriff with a jewel in its navel, and a translucent tulle sheath hand-embroidered with so many birds of paradise in strategic places that you expected the wearer to take wing and fly away. But it was not the get-ups that left a lasting impression.

As soon as they had been seated, the ladies, who had been consistently nipped and tucked to what amounted to perfection, set their purses, like duelling pistols, on the table before them. Putting the faded clutch purse, embroidered and given to me by Laetitia Mercy, above the place card that proclaimed 'Mrs Jordan Flatland' (an appellation I refuted) in ornate copperplate, my mouth dropped open as I looked around me at the circle of purses fashioned entirely from multicoloured rhinestones, each one a work of art. A green and gold frog, a black and white panda, a scarlet bedecked elephant, a purple eggplant, and a bunch of asparagus vied for supremacy. I had seen the ornate reticules in the locked showcase in Neiman Marcus and knew that the cheapest of them must have set the owner back thousands of dollars.

It was a night to remember, but meaningless to Jordan who had spent much of the evening talking shop with Sherman and who had never heard of a Judith Leiber purse.

Successful as she was in her job, Nadine had her problems. Not the least of these were the anorexia to which she did not admit, although she could not have weighed in at more than ninety pounds, her childlessness (she would not hear of adoption) and Sherman's sexual addiction for which he had undergone treatment in an Arizona clinic. In the face of his philandering, which was an open secret, she stood by her man who paradoxically worshipped the ground she stood on. Away from her office — there were few parties in August — Nadine was as bored with Paris as I. We exchanged moans about the garbage and the heat and the fact that we hardly saw our husbands and that when we did they had other things on their minds, and our yearning to be back in the air-conditioned comfort of Boston. My saga about tidying Michelle's room and taking her jeans to be repaired and chauffeuring Joey to his violin lesson and shopping for vegetables in the rue de Buci and getting some lamb chops (his favourite) for Jordan's dinner, elicited a telling silence from the other end of the telephone. I knew that for all her talent and success in business, Nadine would have willingly jettissoned *Anyoccasion.com* for a Joey or a Michelle of her own and a husband who came home at night to eat lamb chops.

With the day looming uninvitingly in front of her, Nadine suggested we continue our dialogue at *A Priori Thé*, in the tranquil backwater of the Gallerie Vivienne where, if you were lucky enough to get a table, you could sit outside, and the chocolate cake, in Nadine's own words — although she only ever picked at it before pushing it to the side of her plate — was 'out of this world'. I told her another time because Jordan wanted dinner early, and that I would call her tomorrow.

Organizing Michelle's room (for which I would get no thanks, she probably wouldn't even notice), and sorting the mêlée of clothes which, if not on the floor, were stuffed indiscriminately into the Louis XIV armoire, occupied me for longer than I had anticipated, and I was on my hands and knees folding sweaters and putting them into neat piles, a task I found inexplicably satisfying, when Joey reminded me that it was time for his music lesson.

I liked Fridays when, while Joey was at Madame Bercot's — 'elbow hup, Joey, elbow hup!' — I could stroll incognito along the *quais*, among the illustrious shades of Sibelius and Hemingway, Camille Pissaro, Molière and Danton. Driving over the Pont du Carrousel, over the muddy waters of the fast flowing Seine, I dropped him off in the Boulevard Saint Germain, then parked illegally on the pavement in the rue Grégoire de Tours.

The rue de Buci — packed with motorbikes, menu-scribbled blackboards, stands of provocatively stockinged plaster legs, carousels of postcards and decorated barrows of torpedo-like sandwiches — was a far cry from the Napoleonic splendour of the Boulevard Courcelles. On the pavement of the Atlas brasserie, late lunchers still lingered over deep plates of mussels, and a line of people in shorts and sandals queued in the doorway of Carton for their evening bread. A chutzpahdik newspaper hawker, hustling copies of *USA Today*, drew smiles from the good-natured crowds with his po-faced and raucous announcement: 'Monica Lewinsky pregnant by George Bush!'

Outside Hamon, beneath the green canopy, the sweet turnips and tender carrots, the field mushrooms and the cherries and the *fraises des bois* were being packed away. Consulting my shopping list and bearing in mind the defunct fridge, I filled my basket with sufficient fruit and vegetables to take us over the weekend.

At the Rôtisserie de Buci, I stood before the *noix de veau*, the *faux filets*, the *magrets de canard*, the purple-tinged *cailles* and minuscule pigeons, lost, as always, in admiration, not only at the form and content, but the passion and artistry which had fashioned the display, as in the finest museum, into a work of art.

'Bonjour, Madame Flatland. How are the fingers?'

I spun round. Félix Dumoulin sat black-clad astride his gleaming Kawasaki at the kerb. Recalling the birthday cake, Joey's trick candles and the glance which had passed between us and which I had tried to forget, I blushed like a young girl.

'The fingers are fine. What are you doing here?'

'I live here.' He inclined his head towards the corner of the rue Dauphine then removed his crash helmet and got off his bike.

'What are *you* doing here?'

I indicated the *boucherie*. 'I come every Friday ... ' Entering the shop and not trusting my schoolgirl French, I pointed, feeling caught out in my least flattering skirt and with my shopping-basket over my arm like a suburban housewife, to some lamb chops in the cabinet amongst the artichokes and radishes and the *herbes de Provence*. 'It's really boring.'

He had followed me into the interior of the

shop where the white-aproned butcher's sharp blade hovered over the chops awaiting my decision as to weight or number. At my nod the cleaver descended.

'Nothing is boring.' There was no cynicism in his voice. The butcher was weighing the meat and wrapping it in white paper.

'Try getting a buzz from a lamb chop.'

Waiting patiently while I stood in line at the cash desk, Félix took the package from me and accompanied me out into the sunlight.

Stopping at Hamon, and unwrapping the white paper, he rescued a few sprigs of rosemary, some flat-leaved parsley, and a bunch of thyme from a disappearing box and placed them on top of the lamb chops.

'I like people who cook,' he said. 'Time people. You can't hurry a soufflé.'

'I could give Jordan stones and he wouldn't notice . . .'

It was true. He was so preoccupied that meals came way down on the agenda, and he often had very little idea what he was eating.

Félix Dumoulin indicated the pavement café. 'Some coffee?'

I looked at my watch and took my car keys from my bag, jiggling them pointedly. 'I have to collect Joey from his music lesson and Jordan wants dinner early.'

'Where is your car?'

We dodged our way among the multitudes, past the vitrines of spectacle frames, the meringue mountains and trays of sushi, the flagons of olive oil and square green cakes of soap. As we passed the riotous display of lys blancs and gerbera, dahlias and hypericum outside the flower shop, Félix plucked a long-stemmed rose from a zinc bucket, smiling conspiratorially as he did so at the *patronne*, a Delft figure in the cool interior, dexterously securing a floral arrangement with a twist of wire.

In the rue Grégoire de Tours, he held open the door of the Renault which was now tightly wedged between a BMW and a Peugeot. When, red in the face, both from heat and embarrassment, and with Félix's encouragement, I had bumped and bounced my way out of the parking spot, I put my head through the open window.

'Thanks for the help.' The perspiration was running down my face.

He placed the rose beneath the wiper on my wind-shield. It was identical to the first.

7

I had promised to take Joey and Andy — who was waiting for us with his Thunderbird convertible and statutory Game Boy — to the Bois de Boulogne. It was Joey's consolation prize. He hated it without Michelle and showed it, even though she had only been gone for a couple of days.

With a lingua franca of Pokemon, baseball, and snippets from the current comics — 'What wobbles and can fly? A jelly copter!' — the two boys got on well and functioned in a world of their own in which I did not figure until they were hungry, thirsty, needed to go to the bathroom or fell and grazed their knees. Sometimes back home I would look at Joey's classmates with their angelic nine-year-old faces, their lustrous hair and their stocky figures and try to predict which among them would be the leaders — the senators, the hotshot lawyers, the wheeler-dealers — and which the led. Nine was such a tender age. Half-boys, half-babies. In no time at all they would be engaged in a long and painful battle, in the grip of the testosterone that would redefine their bodies, alter their sweet voices, dictate their every thought and action rendering it hard to give credence to anything other than their sexual secrets. Joey and Andy, a few yards away, one dark, one fair, in almost identical teeshirts and shorts, Game Boys in hand, engrossed in incomprehensible dialogue to which I listened with half an ear, immured in their Pokemon world, were as happy as extraterrestrial sandboys.

'Where do I find a Rapidash?' The voice was Joey's.

Andy punched a few buttons:

'Find a Ponyta in Pokemon House on Cinnabar Island and raise it to Level 40.'

'I've got the Magikarp Splash. It's scary.'

'It's harmless. Train it 'til it learns Tackle.'

'Where are you now?'

'Level three . . . '

'How do I get to the Sea Cottage? I can get as far as Bill's House . . . '

'Bill's house *is* the Sea Cottage, silly!'

'I'm going to the old man in Viridian City . . . '

'Brock and Ash are having a duel.'

'I'm parched. Can we have an ice-cream?'

I realized that Joey was talking to me, and said that they could go to the kiosk although the ice-cream would melt in moments. Keeping an eye on them from where I sat, I picked up my book.

I don't know quite when it was that I realized I was not alone. It was a feeling one gets, and I looked round to see Félix Dumoulin. I don't know how long he had been there, standing motionless behind me.

'I didn't mean to frighten you.' He was holding his crash-helmet.

'You didn't.'

'May I?' He indicated the bench.

'Of course.' I shuffled along although the seat was empty. 'We had a telephone call this morning from Michelle. She and Lois are in Frankfurt.'

The information went unacknowledged. It was if I had not spoken. He hung his hands between his knees.

'How long will you stay in Paris?'

'Not much longer I hope. It's too hot . . . ' The midday heat was bouncing off the paths. 'My husband — Michelle's father — ' I sounded like a right nerd, 'is buying a company on behalf of a client. The deal is virtually completed.'

'*Tant pis.*'

He looked at the title of my book, which posited that true art was a vital force without which life was scarcely worth living, and raised an eyebrow in surprise.

In answer to his unspoken question I said: 'I majored in art.'

I thought of the years I had spent comparing and contrasting Caravaggio's and Vasari's accounts of Michelangelo and Raphael, explaining what Heidegger meant when he said that 'The art work opens up in its own way the Being of beings', writing essays on the disparate views of Plato and Aristotle.

'I take visitors round the Museum of Fine Arts in Boston. 'Good afternoon, ladies and gentlemen. The gallery we are now standing in is the American gallery . . . Can you hear me at the back? The Boston collection of American art is one of the finest in the country. Please feel free to ask questions. Particularly significant are the colonial and Federal portraits dominated by over sixty works by John Singleton Copley and more than fifty by Gilbert Stuart. Of course we can't see all these in the space of one afternoon . . . ' Pause for laughter. 'The collection also contains an unusually large and fine group of paintings by the romantics and realists of the latter part of the century: Winslow Homer, Thomas Eaking, James NcNeill Whistler, etc . . . ''

Taking the paperback from my hand, Félix glanced at the chapter I was reading: 'The Semiotics of Sex.'

'Not many artists are comfortable with

sex . . . ' I said, listening to myself with horror.

I had written my dissertation on Picasso whose copulating donkeys precociously filled the margins of his schoolbook and whose teenage brothel-going was unflinchingly recorded in his later depictions of perversion and depravity.

'Picasso, of course.' I was unable to stop myself. 'Balthus . . . '

'That pornographer!' His voice was dismissive.

'Bougereau?'

'What Bougereau painted was *desire*: window-shopping. To get sex across you have to decide whether you are a participant or an observer and what it is about the act that permits you to turn it into a work of art.'

'Do you need permission?'

'From yourself. To free you from constraint.'

His English bore the seductive trace of an accent. I wondered what I was doing sweltering on a bench in the Bois de Boulogne discussing the objectivity or subjectivity of sex with a comparative stranger. To my relief, Joey's voice broke into the conversation as, once again, I began to experience bizarre symptoms, a mini heat-wave which had little to do with the overhead sun.

'Mom! We're hungry.'

'You've just had an ice-cream.' The response was conditioned. Looking at my watch, I put the Mona Lisa bookmark that I had picked up at the Louvre firmly into 'The Semiotics of Sex' and closed the book.

'I promised to take them for a pizza.'

'I would like to ask you something Madame Flatland . . . '

Wondering what was coming, I stood up.

'Will you have lunch with me?'

'I'm afraid it's out of the question.'

'How out of the question?'

'I'm a married woman.'

He looked genuinely puzzled.

'Married women have lunch.'

Joey and Andy were getting impatient.

'I'll think about it,' I said, echoing Jordan. 'I'm afraid we have to go now.'

When we got back to the car there was a red rose on the windscreen. I wondered what was going on.

★   ★   ★

I had left Joey sleeping over at Andy's and was having dinner with Jordan, who had been speaking to Sherman on his mobile for the last ten minutes, when the telephone rang in the hall. I was expecting Joey — he usually forgot something.

'Madame Flatland?'

I recognized the voice.

I looked nervously towards the dining-room and turned my back on the ornate glass doors.

'What is it?'

'Have you thought about it?'

'Thought about what?'

'Lunch.' Not giving me a chance to answer, he said, 'Tuesday. Wepler. Place de Clichy. *Midi*.'

There was a click as he put down the phone.

'Who was that?' Forking up the crudités I had prepared — it was too hot for anything else — Jordan's enquiry was perfunctory.

'A friend of Michelle's.'

I had no intention of accepting the invitation to Wepler. Not only was I within a few years of being old enough to be Félix Dumoulin's mother but the whole thing was quite ridiculous. Possessed of a punishing conscience, I had never been good at making up my mind and often left resolutions to Jordan who had the greatest difficulty in tuning in to my vacillations. Last summer, for instance, he had asked me if I wanted to go away at Thanksgiving, or would I rather stay home? The decision was not that important in the grand order of things, but how could I make up my mind about November while we were spending August in Cape Cod? Although Jordan's pencil was not actually poised over his diary nor his fingers over his electronic organizer which was by his side on the sun-deck, I knew that it was a matter of scheduling and that he would be perfectly happy either way.

The dialectic which the question provoked rampaged for several days in my head. As Jordan lay on the lounger outside our beach house, screened from the harmful rays of the sun by the *Wall Street Journal*, he was unaware of the ripples created by the pebble he had dropped into the still waters of my holiday mode, of the far-reaching effects of the innocent enquiry which would last until we got home which was the deadline I had been given.

The argument went something like this. If we stayed home to enjoy the annual round of Thanksgiving parties given by our friends, which we enjoyed, it also entailed eating Thanksgiving dinner with Laetitia which I would do anything to avoid. In an atmosphere so tense you could cut it with a knife, we would be condemned to sit round the long table like corpses at a funeral, waiting for the meal to be served and hoping that Joey would not let us down by disappearing from the table when he got bored.

It was always a long haul. Before dinner there were 'drinks', sweet sherry which Jordan hated, in the un-heated library served by Phillip (his surname), the male half of the couple who had looked after the senior Flatlands since time immemorial. The sherry was accompanied by a Shaker bowl of salted almonds, counted out in the kitchen by Mrs Phillip. In the years since I had known Jordan I had never discovered if Laetitia's cook had another name. While we were drinking the sherry to the accompaniment of conversation so laboured you would take us for strangers, Joey would sit on the very edge of one of the unwelcoming sofas, with a glazed expression on his face, and swing his legs rythmically as if they were metronomes waiting for the tune to be over.

There was never a first course. It was one of the unwritten rules. We sat in our allotted places, Jordan in his father's chair, and remained with our hands in our laps for what seemed an eternity until Phillip staggered in with the turkey which he set solemnly on the buffet as if it were a votive offering. He then returned to the kitchen for the beans, the squash, and the sweet potatoes by which time the turkey was getting cold. Mrs Phillip never helped her husband. Never entered the dining-room. It was not her place. When everything had been brought in, the gravy cooling in its boat, and Phillip satisfied that nothing had been forgotten, he would pick up the ivory-handled carving-knife as if it were a ceremonial sword and set about slicing the not overlarge bird. There was no question of individual preference for the white or the brown meat being voiced, no predilection for skin, dislike of stuffing or requests for the parson's nose. We accepted what we were given, which was never overgenerous, and watched it congeal on the unadorned white plate until everyone had been served.

Once, many years ago, after we had gone home, I had asked Jordan why he did not do the carving. He was not even permitted to pour the wine, which was always extremely good; his father had a first-rate cellar. Jordan had laughed. Upsetting the apple-cart of his mother's routine was unthinkable. It was not worth the hassle.

Delicious as the turkey was — Mrs Phillip was no mean cook — there was never any question of second helpings. No sooner had we put down our knives and forks than the remains would be carried away as ceremoniously as they had been served and the buffet cleared. During the hiatus — Phillip was not exactly a ball of fire when it came to clearing the table — we did not actually 'talk amongst ourselves' so much as eavesdrop on Jordan reminiscing about old times with his mother, conversation from which Michelle, Joey and myself were excluded. If the discussion did become general, one had to remember that despite the fact that Jordan made his living from it, money was a no-go area and must never be mentioned.

The Thanksgiving turkey, like every other meal at 'Beacon Hill' (as we always referred to Jordan's mother's house) was followed by fresh fruit, not in a common fruit bowl but each variety set separately on individual plates arranged tastefully on the table. Mangoes, passion-fruit, pineapple, oranges, grapes, kiwis, pears, lychees, bananas and papayas, each one at the peak of its perfection. This largesse was not as profligate as it appeared. Any leftovers were used to make the large bowl of fruit salad which would sustain Laetitia, even in the depths of winter, for the remainder of the week. At my mother-in-law's table, in the early days of my marriage to Jordan, I learned the correct way to tackle a mango, how to eject the seeds from a passion-fruit, and to eat a banana with a knife and fork slicing it longitudinally for maximum flavour.

Brought up in this atmosphere of unassailable protocol, it was surprising that Jordan had turned out to be as normal as he was. I attributed this to his strength of character — he assessed everything for himself from first principles and was not easily swayed — and glimpsed vestiges of the Flatland programming only in his ordered thinking and his loathing of fresh fruit in any shape or form.

Whether or not to accept Félix Dumoulin's invitation was hardly something I could discuss with Jordan. The debate, like the Thanksgiving one, was with myself. The issue was simple. Was I going to turn up at the brasserie or was I not? At one point I thought of involving Lauren and one evening, while Jordan, in a brief moment of reprieve from Rochelle Eléctronique, played Red Sox Monopoly on the floor with Joey, I crossed the corridor and rang her bell. She answered the door with the mobile at her ear — like Jordan, Lauren was forever on the phone — and motioning me to enter indicated that she would not be long. Whilst our rented apartment was seemingly untouched by the march of time, Lauren's, which was paid for by a long-time lover — a wealthy but impotent French aristocrat who in return for her life-enhancing company kept her in style and asked no questions — had been modernized over the years. Looking at myself in one of the many mirrors in which were reflected the white sofas, the oversize flower arrangements, the Miro above the chimney-piece, the glass table littered with sketches and colour-swatches, the copies of *Vogue* and the bottle of red wine which was never far from Lauren's side, I examined my face, as if the secret of Félix Dumoulin's interest in me was hidden in my countenance. All I could see in the oval contours, the green eyes, the idiosyncratic indentation between nose and lip and the upswept hair, was a mature version of Michelle to whom I had bequeathed the first flush of my youth.

Lauren was haranguing one of her suppliers, this time in German. Although languages were not her forte, she spoke several of them fluently and with the contempt she considered any attention to grammar deserved. Marching round the room she poured herself a drink and raised a questioning eyebrow at me, which I answered in the negative, without interrupting her guttural flow. I wondered what Lauren would make of my invitation to Wepler and what her advice would be, but the moment she had finished with Germany, her mobile, with its Overture from William Tell, rang again. Chickening out — there was nothing after all to *tell* Lauren, and I had to make up my own mind about Wepler — I blew her a kiss and was gone.

In the end it was curiosity, although I knew that this was not strictly honest, which won the day.

8

I dared not risk finding somewhere to park in the Place de Clichy, and there had been problems getting a taxi. Unlike Jordan, Félix Dumoulin seemed not to be agitated by my tardiness and did not even appear to be wearing a watch beneath his unbuttoned cuffs. Standing up at my approach, he kissed me politely on both cheeks. I apologized for being late and explained about the taxi.

'Did you think I wouldn't come?'

'I'm happy that you did.'

There was a bottle of Mersault on the table into which he had made inroads. He filled my glass, and I took advantage of the moment to look around me at the noisy lunch-time crowd, anxious lest I should bump into anyone I knew. To conceal my agitation I filled him in with the minutiae of my days since our last meeting, a blow-by-blow account of the progress of Jordan's deal and Joey's exploits and Michelle's current where-abouts — there had been a postcard from Bruges, at which he nodded gravely as if my nervous soliloquy was a matter of conse-quence. By the time we picked up the menus

I was surprised to find that we had finished the Mersault and that more than half an hour had passed.

It wasn't like that with Jordan for whom time was of the essence and who did not like to linger over a meal or to be kept waiting for his food.

'One comes here for the *fruits de mer*.'

Jordan was not keen on seafood. He liked his fish more easily accessible and, although he did his best to hide it, grew impatient while I picked at winkles, opened moules or entered the lobster jousts.

Over the vast crustacean still life on its glacier of ice which was brought ceremoniously to the table along with triangles of brown bread and butter, lemon halves, glossy pots of mayonnaise and the tools of icthyoid torture, we left Jordan and Joey and the whereabouts of Michelle. Assisted by a second bottle of wine, I held forth about my life in Boston and my job at the Museum of Fine Arts which I had touched upon in the Bois de Boulogne. Félix was not impressed. Looking at paintings, he said, was a skill that must be learned. Art could not be appreciated on the trot, and hurrying visitors through crowded galleries was inimical to developing a proper rapport with any particular work.

'You have to fall in love with a painting, Madame Flatland . . . '

'Judith.'

'You have to fall in love with a painting, Judith.'

I liked the way he said my name.

'It's like falling in love with a woman . . . '

He held my gaze, and as the avuncular waiters and the boisterous party of young people at the next table faded from view, I thought that I was going to have another of my dizzy spells.

'A painting needs to be looked at single-mindedly, for its own sake. How many people look at a picture honestly? How many people allow the image to speak for itself?'

He was right, of course. Increasingly the galleries had a habit of advertising when they had acquired a particular exhibit and how much it had cost. While many of the observers saw not the colours on the canvas but the colour of money, others were interested only if the artist — or the work itself — was famous, in which case they would admire it or reject it on principle.

We had finished the *fruits de mer* down to the last *bigorneau*, and were discussing the current obsession with the past which sometimes made the work of new artists seem out of synch.

'If you love a Velazquez you can love a Bacon,' Félix said. 'If you *really* love a Velazquez. Do you like my city, Judith?'

'I love your city — ' I loved the teeming streets, the vibrancy ' — but I miss my friends. And my utility room.'

'Utility room?'

'Where you do the washing . . . and the ironing . . . and keep things: tools . . . and muddy boots . . . '

'A fairy princess. Shut away in her castle. And what about Prince Charming?'

'What about him?'

'When did he last see his princess?'

'This morning.'

'See her? Or look at her, like his Rolex?'

If a loved one is well known enough there is no need to look at him. It was an axiom of married life. I felt the need to defend Jordan.

'It wasn't always like that.' I glanced at my watch. 'I have to collect Joey from karate.'

'Jordan. Joey. What about Judith?'

'I promised to take him to the cinema. *Toy Story 2* . . . '

'Toys which come alive when human beings are not around?'

I looked at him in surprise. 'It's a kid's movie!'

'It taps into primal emotions. Emotions which everyone can relate to.'

'Toys being outgrown?'

'If you're a child and you're lost, someone will find you. If you're broken, you can be fixed. Being outgrown is the worst thing that can happen to a toy. It isn't really *about* toys . . . '

I imagined having this conversation with Jordan.

'What is it about?'

'About the fear of growing up, about the fear of getting older . . . ' He looked straight at me. 'About the fear of your children leaving home.' He broke off as a flower seller who was working the restaurant approached our table. Plucking a red, cellophane-wrapped rose from her basket, he laid it on my plate.

'For the Empress Josephine . . . '

'The Empress Josephine?' It was hard to keep up with him.

'She consoled herself with roses, at Malmaison. After her divorce from Napoleon.'

Picking up the rose, I felt its broad-based thorns through the paper. Not for the first time, I wondered what he wanted with me.

'*J'ai envie de coucher avec toi.*'

I should of course have got up and left the restaurant there and then. That I did not do so was due not so much to the fact that once again he had read my thoughts nor that he wanted to sleep with me, but the shock that the statement engendered. *Autres temps, autres moeurs.* I was aware, who could not be, that times had changed and that the young people of today fell into bed at will, women as well as men, with no commitment.

'I have a husband . . . ' Meeting Félix's gaze, I was aware from the difficulty I had with the sibilant, that the Mersault was having its effect. 'This deal is important to Jordan. If he pulls it off he gets a seat on the board. If he doesn't . . . '

'If he doesn't?'

'It will destroy him. I also have two children and I am old enough . . . ' Hoping he would not finish the sentence for me, I let the words hang in the air.

★ ★ ★

Rendered soporific by the wine which I was unused to drinking in the middle of the day, I fell asleep in the cinema although Joey, fascinated by the antics of Buzz Lightyear and Woody seemed not to notice.

I didn't hear from Félix for a week. Every time the telephone rang and Jordan picked it up I thought it might be him and spent the next few moments in a paroxysm of anxiety. I wasn't sure if I wanted it to be Félix or not. My rational self told me not to be so idiotic, then I'd remember the kiss he had imprinted on my mouth as he held my face between his hands outside the restaurant. There had been nothing funny about that.

On Sunday, Jordan, in a rare moment of leisure, volunteered to take Joey and Andy to the Cité des Sciences while I went to the marché aux puces with Lauren whose previous night's date had admitted to having a wife and three children, unless it was three wives and two children, she couldn't be quite sure.

Normally I loved wandering round the flea market, keeping my eye open for bargains and trying to picture how my purchases were going to look once I got back to Boston, which now seemed imminent. Pottering amongst the trestle-tables of furniture, bric-à-brac, china, and second-hand clothes I feigned interest in an antique plate but found myself unable to concentrate on it. I enquired as to the price from the hard-faced young stall-holder who had a dragonfly etched on her breast and a cigarette suspended from the corner of her mouth.

'Your Joey is older than this plate.' Lauren removed it gently from my hand.

I pointed to a miniature gramophone. The

girl wound it up for me and we listened to the tinny tune.

Turning over the price ticket I stared at it blankly.

The girl flicked her ash on to the ground.

'Do you want it or not . . . ?' Lauren said. 'Are you feeling all right?'

I wondered should I tell her about Félix but the words stuck in my throat.

My concentration did not improve over the next few days. I took Joey swimming and forgot his trunks and went out without my keys. Staring idly at the bargains in a '*soldes*' window in the Place Sulpice, I heard the approaching noise of a motor-bike and caught sight of a Kawasaki reflected in the glass. I spun round eagerly to see a pimply faced black-clad courier retrieve a package from his box. I searched high and low for Jordan's memo-machine which I had inadvertently tidied away, put salt instead of sugar on my raspberries and glanced involuntarily at the empty wind-shield when I approached my car.

I spent a day in the airy galleries of the Musée d'Orsay. A museum should not be like an encyclopaedia, giving an objective and impersonal account of itself, but should reflect the tastes and choices as well as the blind spots and oversights of the collectors and curators who have built up the corpus over the years. The identity of the Musée d'Orsay was not yet fully established but the excitement of its infancy — the fact that many major artists were unrepresented and entire schools were dealt with inadequately, notwithstanding — never failed to please me.

Looking at paintings with Jordan, on the rare occasions I managed to persuade him into a gallery, was like running after a bus. Art for him was the making of an acquisition or the creation of a new company. The humanities did not exist. In the early days of our marriage he had made a genuine effort. Standing him before a landscape I would attempt to get him to see the effects of light on water, the symbolism of objects, the finesse of a palette, to hear the music the artist was trying to convey. Try as he would to make some sense of what I was on about, I had eventually to give his artistic education up as a bad job. It was a hopeless task. Similarly he would talk to me for hours about fees and mergers and the state of the Dow Jones. No sooner had he started than my mind would seize up and the words would bounce off me. Although his expertise paid for our lifestyle and his business acumen shored us up against privation, I could not tune into it and he could have been speaking

Chinese. This diversity of interests did not mean that we did not love each other. Our various preoccupations added richness and spice to our marriage and whilst we did not understand them, we took vicarious pride in each other's achievements.

I got home from the museum to find an agitated Jordan putting shirts and ties into a bag on the bed. Before I had a chance to ask it he answered my unspoken question.

'Lafarge is playing silly buggers! He has been advised that what we are offering for Rochelle is not enough . . . '

'I thought you'd already come to an agreement with Lafarge?'

'Exactly. His financial advisor has had the temerity to demand an extra five per cent! I'm going to Monte Carlo to find out what he's up to.'

'Why can't his financial advisor come here?' I had the feeling that just at this moment I needed Jordan at home.

'Refuses point blank.' I could see that he was angry. 'I shouldn't be gone more than a couple of days. Sorry darling . . . ' He took me briefly in his arms looking at his watch over my shoulder. 'Be an angel and call a taxi.'

★ ★ ★

Two days later I was in the rue de Buci, trying to concentrate on the aubergines and bell-peppers, and visiting the oil emporium for Lauren; I had promised to buy her a cake of her favourite soap.

I was about to put a melon in my basket when I heard the roar of a Kawasaki but did not look round. The bike came to a halt behind me and Félix appeared, blotting out the sun, by my side. He kissed me on both cheeks.

'I owe you an apology, Judith. I've been in Alsace. My grandmother was taken ill.' He nodded towards an empty table at the crowded bar on the opposite corner. '*Un café?*'

Rooted to the spot, I did not reply.

'I suppose Jordan wants dinner early?'

'Jordan's in Monte Carlo.'

'What brings you to the rue de Buci?'

'I told you, I always come on Friday.'

Taking the melon from my hand, Félix replaced it with another which he held to his nose before placing it gently in my basket.

'Today is Thursday.'

9

I am forty-two years old and knew exactly what I was doing when I went back with Félix to his apartment which looked out on to the terracotta chimney-pots and flower-filled balconies of the rue Dauphine and the rue St André des Arts. There were a lot of things I could have put it down to: the city and its heat, Dr Katz's reference to my age — lumping me together with a whole bunch of neurotic women and isolating me from the human race — Jordan's preoccupation with Rochelle Eléctronique, the fact that I missed my friends and my colleagues at the Museum of Fine Arts. Perhaps the main reason was to do with my feelings vis-à-vis Michelle. It was not so much that I envied her — although of course I did — her youth, her looks, the insouciance with which she appeared to face the world (although I'd been there myself and knew it was a lie), but the fact that she was starting out on a road which as far as I was concerned was well travelled and that her life, no matter what its vicissitudes, unlike mine which was mapped out, had yet to come.

I had been expecting an attic, louche and

bohemian, strewn with canvases and daubed with paint. In nineteenth-century Paris, artists who lived on a few francs a day had congregated in the cafés where they formed an alliance against the world. Later, of course, attracted by the wine, women and hallucinogenic drugs of *la vie de bohème*, cubists, fauvists, Dadaists, surrealists and others (many of whom were to suffer for their art) gravitated towards the twenty-four seven city and settled in Montmartre where they practised free love with their models, smoked opium and drank themselves stupid. Consorting with gangsters and brothel-keepers, and unable to differentiate between freedom and licence, they were quick to pick fights with anyone who crossed their paths, and satisfied their sexual cravings in the knocking-shops of Pigalle. Among the influx of itinerant painters lured to the Citadel of Pleasure from Spain, Italy, Russia and Mexico, Picasso — who together with his mistresses abused all manner of substances in his mice-infested studio — could lay claim to being the most unruly. Never without his revolver, he was well-known for his tendency to fire it over the heads of anyone who annoyed him.

Félix's apartment, beyond a heavy door which opened at the touch of a punched code, was reached by a waxed parquet staircase with decorative iron banisters. With its scrubbed wooden table, its simple vase of white arum lilies, its plan-chest bearing pots of sharpened pencils, old cigar boxes of pastels, containers of linseed oil and fixative, and neatly stacked canvases, it was tranquil and ordered.

While Félix disappeared into the kitchen, I circumvented the studio with its well-used furniture, its overflowing bookshelves, and its sepia prints of erstwhile Paris. I could see no signs of a woman's presence, not even in the bedroom which was visible through the open door. On an easel, which stood near the window, a painting was half-completed. A girl with flaxen hair and virginal breasts lay serenely on a sofa — Félix's sofa with its Indian throw — bathed in gold light.

Returning with a bottle of champagne and following my gaze, Félix answered my unspoken question.

'Olympe . . . '

Olympe. The fragile image of classical beauty shone from the canvas with clarity and tenderness.

'She was my girlfriend.'

'Was?'

There was a moment's hesitation.

'We split up.'

While he took two glasses from a cupboard

and set them on the table beside the arum lilies, he filled me in about his visit to Alsace where his grandmother, who was making a good recovery, had survived her *crise de coeur*. Only partly listening and drinking as slowly as possible, I used the hiatus to access my thoughts, which as usual were a jumble of contradiction, and decide whether or not I was going to make my escape while the going was good or whether I was going to cross the line that separated fantasy from reality. What could I get from this young man with his black shirt and black hair that I did not get from my tall and handsome husband? Why should I compromise my life, my marriage, for a moment of distraction? Should I sacrifice my good name to satisfy the callous appetites of youth? If I did, was it, in today's climate, such a big deal?

Had I not needed to use the bathroom I might have run away. As it was, when I came out, having looked at my face in the mirror above the wash-basin for a long time as if I would find the answer in my pale reflection, Félix was leaning against the table, his dark eyes fixed on the doorway through which I would emerge. Drawn, as by a magnet and freed of inhibition by the alcohol, I moved deliberately towards him until there was no space between us and I could feel the pressure of his firm body, then the warmth of his mouth and the unmistakeable essence of him inviting me, as in the best novels, the finest plays, to abandon the security of my life and deceive my husband, my best friend, the person with whom I shared my confidences, and make a mockery of our marriage. The trouble was that although it was neither a novel nor a play, I managed, throwing caution to the winds and without too much trouble, to overcome my reservations, to give up everything, including myself, and to suspend disbelief.

Any attempt to describe the act of love is like trying to convey the flavour of a particular food to one who has never tasted it. Only those concerned know how love was, how it is, how it will be; the sensations, even the sequence of events, have never been satisfactorily communicated. Not even by a film maker. Particularly not by a film maker, who disregards awkwardness, and odours, and bodily fluids, and cheats on takes, on camera angles and on anatomical truth.

I was aware of my body, divested slowly of its summer dress, its scanty undergarments, and compared its contours, scored with the stretch marks of child-bearing, with the youthful voluptuousness of the girl in the painting as she lay on the sofa with her milkwhite breasts. Abandoned, on the same chaise longue — we drifted later towards the bedroom where a reprise brought sharply home the youth of my lover — I was hard put to say whether the joyful orchestrations which followed the andante and the allegretto, the scherzo and the ode to joy, came from my own lips or through the open shutters from the street below. There was no need to testify on oath about the whispered confidences and tender endearments that passed between us, nor would they be required to stand the test of time. It was not until it was over that I realized I had for once been listening to the music we were making rather than concentrating on a metaphorical chandelier.

It was Carl Jung who said, 'The meeting of two personalities is like the contact of two chemical substances. If there's any reaction, both are transformed.' We lay amongst the twisted sheets, bathed in the afternoon sun. Félix's arm, carpeted with the curls that overflowed from his deep chest, was around me, his firm shoulder smelled sweet. Jordan and Joey and the fact that the engineer was due shortly with the long-awaited part for the refrigerator had receded into the distance. My lover — I had a lover — was kissing my eyes and my nose, vindicating Jung, as I contemplated my altered state.

I sat up on my elbow and ran my fingers through his lustrous hair. 'What exactly is this all about?'

Looking into his eyes, I waited for his protestation, if not of love, of desire.

Rising from the bed with the agility of youth, he moved to the window, light and shade dappling his back. For a long time he was silent, then he turned to face me.

'It was a wager . . . ' he said. 'Alexandre made it at Michelle's birthday party. It was a bet.'

'A bet! What kind of a bet?' So much for Jung. I covered myself with the sheet. Whereas a moment ago I had felt extremely pleased with myself, as if I had passed some sort of test, I now felt cheap, ravaged, manipulated, used.

'At Michelle's party. We had too much to drink. You were dancing with your husband. Alexandre said . . . '

I waited. Félix looked uncomfortable.

'What did Alexandre say?'

''I bet you can't pull the mother instead of the daughter.''

'And you said?'

''What do you bet?''

'And Alexandre said?'

''A case of champagne.''

A case of champagne! I could not speak.

Not looking at him, I got out of his bed and into my trembling dress. He tried to put his arms around me. I pushed him away.

'You're despicable!'

'I come from a long line of gamblers . . . '

'Spare me the excuses.' I picked up my purse. My eyes blinded with tears of humiliation I made for the front door.

'Wait! Judith! There's something I want to say to you . . . '

'Haven't you said enough?'

Félix was pulling on his chinos.

I slammed the front door behind me.

'Enjoy your champagne!'

Rushing blindly up the five flights of stairs in the Boulevard Courcelles, it did not sink in that the *en panne* notice had disappeared and that the elevator had been mended. In the bath, the taps full on, wiping away my hot tears and letting the tepid water run over my breasts to expunge my shame, I felt used, soiled, disgusted with myself. In the space of a few short hours, I had sullied my marriage and all that I had invested in it.

When Jordan came back from Monte Carlo with a Pokedex electronic notebook for Joey and an outsize bottle of Boucheron for me which compounded my guilt, he was full of his encounter with Lafarge's financial advisor.

'If you want to know something, darling,' he said as he unpacked his bag, stowing away his belongings with his customary precision, 'Lafarge's financial adviser is an out and out shit.'

He was not the only one.

'He tried to tell us that we were buying him out on a prospective P\E ratio of 20 when it should be 21 at the very least. I told him, in no uncertain terms, that it was a bit late in the day to challenge the price and that one hell of a lot of money would need to be spent on research and development which would be an enormous strain on the cash flow. In the end — ' I was having difficulty in following the sequence of events ' — they agreed to do a few more sums but I refused to hang around. I said I had to get back to Paris. I left the ball in his court.' He closed the zipper triumphantly. 'He's going to come back to me as soon as he can. What have you been up to, darling?'

Feigning a headache, for which he offered to get me a couple of Tylanol, I avoided his outstretched arms.

*   *   *

I had promised to take Joey to the Luxembourg Gardens. He reminded me at

117

breakfast where he was reading a postcard from his grandmother in Florida.

'Grandma's going to bring me a new skateboard — '

My mother and Walter were due at the weekend.

' — with Santa Cruz wheels and a Powell Peralta deck.'

There was another postcard. From Michelle in Florence. The naked image on the front was Michelangelo's triumphant and analytical recreation of the male human body; David, in his muscular and sensuous prime, carved with three chisels from single piece of marble. It was as if she knew.

The grass in the Luxembourg was yellowed and dry. If we didn't get some rain soon everything would perish. I was sitting on a green chair by the Bassin watching a fascinated Joey urging on his hired boat with his stick, when a red rose landed on my lap. It was unbelievable. I picked it up, pricking my finger on its thorns, and ground it into the gravel as hard as I could with my sandaled foot. I did not look round. I did not need to. I knew that Félix was there.

'How can you have the effrontery . . . ' Passers-by would think I was talking to myself. Standing up, I signalled to Joey. Intent on getting boat number three to the other side of the pond — he had Jordan's determination, an insatiable desire to succeed — he did not see me.

'Judith . . . '

Félix's voice, with its trace of accent, was sonorous and sad. Coming round to where I stood he put a restraining hand on my arm. I pulled it away.

'Let me go.'

'There is something I have to say.'

I put my hands over my ears.

'About the champagne . . . '

'You won your bet. Now leave me alone.'

I looked straight ahead at the foreign visitors, at the Japanese with their cameras, at the fathers carrying toddlers on their shoulders, at the groups of excited children liberated from school, at Joey who was racing round the stone perimeter of the pond.

'Look, Mom!' Boat number three had reached the other side.

'Fantastic! We have to go now Joey.'

'I couldn't sleep . . . '

'Tough.'

'I wanted to explain about the wager . . . '

'I really don't want to know.'

Making my way towards a triumphant Joey who, flushed with pride, was hauling his boat out of the water, I resisted the temptation, as if I were at risk of being transformed into a pillar of salt, to glance behind me. When I did look round, Félix had gone.

★ ★ ★

Had it not been for Claude Lafarge and the fact that Jordan became totally immersed in Rochelle Eléctronique, had my mother and Walter not come at the opportune moment to whisk Joey away to Scotland, had it not been for the intolerable heat sending me slightly stir-crazy, that might have been that. I would have to live with my perfidy: everyone is entitled to one indiscretion. Looked at with hindsight and in the light of contemporary mores, my afternoon with Félix was not such a big deal.

On the day my mother was due, as he was about to leave the apartment for his office at Offenbach Fréres, Jordan received a call from Monte Carlo. From the satisfied look on his face I could tell — and learned later that my assumption was correct — that his negotiations with Lafarge's financial advisor had been successful and that as far as the extra 5 per cent was concerned the Ministry of Defence had backed down.

My mother was one of the many thousands of GI brides who had, despite parental opposition, left the school in the Devon

120

village to which she had been evacuated during World War Two and sailed away to New York with the good-looking medical corps sergeant, who later became a popular and caring physician and ultimately, almost after they had given up hope of having a baby, my father. At the age of seventy-four, all traces of her English upbringing had been eradicated and you would have been forgiven for mistaking her for a native American. Contrary to expectations, the marriage had succeeded, due largely, I suspect, to my mother's grit and perseverance and her determination to work in order to put my father through medical school.

Unqualified for anything, she had taken a job as a cosmetics saleswoman with a start-up firm that had no visible retail presence but was later to become a multi-million dollar company operating in more than a hundred countries and quoted on the New York stock exchange. Travelling more than 500 miles a week, she sold hair care, skin care and toiletries to lonely housewives who regarded her as a friend — she knew every cat and dog by name — and looked forward to her visits as much as they did the foundations and fragrances, the lotions and nail enamel, in their distinctive purple packaging which she produced from her bag. Although life on the road was hard and the rewards derisory, one of them had to earn the bread-and-butter and my mother was quite content to do so. When questioned now, she would protest that the products sold themselves. Sometimes however, despite her best efforts and enthusiasm, the customers ordered nothing at all, or at best a stick of deodorant or a single eyeshadow, and she invented her own little ploys to increase sales and combat rejection. Faced with a client who seemed reluctant to put her hand in her purse for a new product, she would ask if there was an eggcup in the house and cunningly leave a free sample of bubble bath or shower gel to be tried out at leisure. As the firm prospered so did my mother. She rose from sales rep to area manager and later to general manager with shares in the company. Once my father had qualified she could of course have retired but by that time she was so hooked on the cosmetics that it had become a way of life and she a valued member of the organization.

We were a tight knit and happy little family and when my father died from lung cancer when I was ten — due probably to his wartime smoking — my mother was totally devastated. Showing the same determination as she had when she married him however, she had carried on working to keep us both in relative comfort and, unable to stop, had continued even after I was married. A few years ago she had met Walter who had prevailed upon her to give up what was now more a crusade than a career, and move with him to Florida. While my father had had charisma, and I fully understood why my mother's seventeen-year-old head had been turned, Walter had none. A neatly dressed short man with a balding head and a grey moustache, he lacked the positive attributes of my father and having never been married, which struck me as suspect, he was interested in very little apart from golf and fishing.

I understood why my mother had thrown in her lot with Walter. Life as a widow could not have been exactly a whole bunch of laughs, and with her only daughter living so far away, she must have felt increasingly lonely. Whether sex came into the equation I did not know and could hardly ask. If it did I doubt that the earth moved as by all accounts it had with my father, and the only chemistry I could detect between them, if chemistry there was, was my mother's occasionally reassuring hand with its brown age spots over his, his overwhelming generosity towards her and his touching concern for her well-being.

Wrapped up in her work and her passionate affair with my father, which by all accounts seemed never to have gone stale, my mother and I, who got on well enough, had never been particularly close. When I married Jordan, we did not see too much of each other although we kept in touch. I think she thought that I had been infected with the Flatland snobbery and kept her distance, even on her rare visits to Boston, which she associated with a milieu to which she could never aspire even had she wanted to, which she did not.

Unlike Laetitia Flatland, she could not tune into Michelle to whom in her opinion we allowed too much freedom — as if in today's climate of youth culture we could do anything else — and it was only after Joey was born that she began to take her grandmother role seriously. Perhaps, with his sunny disposition, it was because there was more than a passing resemblance to his maternal grandfather, perhaps because Joey represented the son she had always wanted but had never had, I don't know. Whatever it was, she was besotted with her only grandson and her feelings were reciprocated. The highlight of Joey's year was the part of the summer vacation that he spent with Grandma Pam and Walter. The latter had not only infected Joey with a passion for fishing, but had managed to convince him that he would be catching his dream trout with every fly he tied. This year they were taking him to a lodge beside the river Tey in Scotland. You would not think that a boy of ten would relish the prospect of three weeks standing in the water in a pair of thigh-waders, in the company of a couple as old as my mother — still a walking advert for her products with her wrinkle-free skin and 'President's Red' lipstick — and Walter, but Joey could hardly wait.

10

They had arrived an hour late at Charles de Gaulle airport both anxiously pushing a loaded trolley on which, apart from the matching suitcases and Burberry raincoats in anticipation of the rain in Scotland, were two sets of golf sticks — my mother had taken up the game at Walter's instigation — Walter's fishing tackle, including a two-handed rod for Joey, and Joey's skateboard.

Looking at my mother's trim figure, her honey-coloured Palm Beach trouser suit matching her honey-coloured shoes and her honey-coloured hair — since marrying Walter she had metamorphosed into Palm Beach woman — I thought that she could easily have been taken for twenty years younger.

We were in the middle of dinner. My mother was removing every scrap of fat from Walter's steak in the interests of his cholesterol, and entertaining Joey with stories about what life in England had been like when she was his age. She was telling him how children were unafraid to play in the streets or roam on their own in the fields, and she and Walter were trying to think about all the things everyone takes for granted these days that weren't around when she was a child, when the telephone rang at the same moment as Jordan's mobile.

'I'll get it.' Excusing myself from the table I ran into the hall as my mother muttered something to the effect that having dinner with the Flatlands was akin to eating in Grand Central Station.

'Hallo?'

'I just wanted to hear your voice. I'm outside your apartment. *J'ai besoin de t'embrasser.*'

I slammed down the receiver and going back into the dining-room, tried abortively, my hand shaking, to pour myself some mineral water.

'You have to open it, dear!' Sharp-eyed as ever, my mother indicated the plastic stopper which was still in the bottle as I upended it over my glass. Jordan, anxious to tell me his news, made no comment.

'That was Sherman, honey. The MOD has backed down. They're ready to sign . . . '

'Brilliant.'

'P/E ratios. Contingent liabilities. I've never heard such crap!'

I heard the sound of a Kawasaki in the street below and pushed my plate away, the steak half-finished.

' . . . dishwashers, tumble-driers, electric blankets . . . ' my mother was saying brightly. She looked at Walter.

'Ballpoint pens, credit cards . . . '

'Frozen foods, easy-care . . . '

'Penicillin, polio shots . . . '

'Scotch tape . . . '

'Contact lenses . . . '

'Post-it notes . . . '

'Artificial hearts . . . '

'Electricity!' The voice was Joey's.

'I'm not *that* old, dear!'

'Radar, split atoms, laser beams, space travel, micro-chips, fax machines, automatic transmission, parking meters . . . ' Always the perfect host, Jordan took his mind off Sherman, Claude, and P\E ratios and joined in the game. 'Mobile phones, Xerox, scanners, the internet, CDs, DVDs, video recorders . . . ' The words came out in quick succession.

'Robot-chefs, plastic bags, detergents . . . Can't *you* think of anything, Judith?'

'Sorry?'

'Aren't you going to join in?'

I wondered if there was anything that could dispel the guilt and remorse with which I was consumed.

'Viagra,' Walter said. I looked at him sharply.

'I asked *Judith*, Walter.'

'Disposable diapers.' It was all I could think of.

While my mother explained to Joey how in her day babies' diapers, which were made of terry-towelling, had to be boiled in a wash-boiler before putting them through a mangle — a word with which Joey was unfamiliar — and hanging them on a line in the backyard, I was thinking about Félix. I could not get him out of my mind.

'Penny for them, Judith.' My mother's voice broke into my reverie. She turned to Jordan. 'Judith's looking very pale. She's not herself. Why don't you take her down to that villa in the South of France you were telling us about? Just the two of you. While Joey's away.'

With the contracts for Rochelle Eléctronique as yet unsigned, a vacation was the last thing on Jordan's mind.

Next morning, while my mother and Walter slept off their jet lag, I finished packing Joey's case, not forgetting his one-eyed teddy-bear — he was still a baby really — then took him with his new skateboard, dodging the traffic and skirting the rows of parked cars, across the road to the Parc Monceau. He couldn't wait to try out his grandmother's present.

Inside the iron gates, letting go of my hand,

Joey raced ahead, leaving me to stroll among the young mothers with their baby buggies, the chic Embassy children with their chic minders, the babies in the swing enclosure, the oblivious lovers obstructing the paths as they stopped to kiss, to a cool seat beneath the tropical palms, where, amid the families making the most of the long hot summer, I could keep an eye on him.

Having been brought up with a minimalist one of my own — my father's early death; my mother's siblings in England — I was a strong believer in the family unit which despite all attempts to destroy it had somehow managed to survive. Not merely a human phenomenon nor an artificial social construct, the family went deeper than reason and was part of nature itself. Although many people were able to manage perfectly well on their own, and often preferred to do so, there was something within the human spirit that seemed to crave the ties of kinship. Current trends were ephemeral, instinct was not. Watching Joey with his new skateboard which had attracted a posse of similarly aged admirers, I thought of the male bird bringing food to his fledgelings, the lioness scavenging for her cubs. Both were obeying an atavistic imperative.

While propagation of the species was a

basic need and offspring often a central part of the configuration, the family was not defined by it. Sex and procreation existed independently, and while the family certainly contained these elements it also went beyond them. Many societies had tried to disrupt, or at least weaken, the power of the family. They trotted out any number of reasons, one of which was that the emotional and practical restraints within the group hampered individual growth. There was little doubt that taking care of children, providing for them and having to pay attention to a spouse, while emotionally satisfying, consumed vast quantities of time and energy. If the family did not endorse these occupations, it was hard to be a great writer, a round the world yachtswoman or a dedicated breeder of rare orchids, while cooking three meals a day, teaching children to read, supervising homework, shopping for groceries, feeding a dog, picking up the kids from school and attending parent-teacher meetings.

There were many different images of 'the family', some of them downright sentimental. The most romantic notion, perpetuated by Hollywood, pulp fiction, and some womens' magazines, insisted that kinship was synonymous with affection and the family synonymous with love. Nothing was further from the truth. Family members often heartily disliked each other and the home was by no means always the haven it was cracked up to be. Extreme closeness was not a blueprint for happiness — sometimes it was just the opposite — but it did at least ensure the creation of a unique relationship. Knowing someone from infancy established a bond that could never be broken. An alliance existed among family members which marked their obligations to each other and endorsed an unwritten contract that was based on trust.

The entwined couples enjoying the sunshine in the Allée de la Comtesse de Ségur, were concerned not so much with family ties as with the urge to procreate, a compelling drive which did not necessarily encompass feelings. Male and female fish, as I had observed from watching Joey's guppies, had an elaborate courtship ritual and strange reproductive habits; they did not so much as touch each other and fertilization occurred outside their bodies. Their enjoyment of the sex act, if it existed, came from fulfilling the compulsion and not from tactile pleasure.

'Judith . . . '

The voice of my lover, low-pitched and resonant, broke into my wandering thoughts. Taken by surprise and aware of my burning cheeks I called to Joey who turned towards me for a moment then went back to his skateboard. He never came the first time.

'I need to talk to you.'

'Please go away.'

'It's about the wager . . . '

'Joey!'

'I would like to explain.'

'Stop pestering me.' Getting up I walked towards the gated enclosure where two little girls in a double swing, watched by their long-suffering mother, were soaring into the air and laughing.

'It started long before the wager.'

I looked involuntarily at my hand to where the candle had burned my finger.

'When you walked into Wepler . . . It had nothing to do with cases of champagne, nothing to do with Alexandre.'

'*Regarde, Maman! Regarde!*'

The swing was going higher and higher.

'*Doucement, chérie, doucement.*'

'You've done something to me Judith. I think of you, dream of you. I'm not making a very good job of this . . . '

'Joey!'

Joey looked round bemusedly.

'Pick up your skateboard. We're going home.'

'Mom!'

'I'm sorry about the wager and I'd really like to see you again.'

'Forget it.'

'Look Mom!'

Joey was executing an 'Ollie Airwalk', jumping off his new skateboard and, doing a half-turn, landing on it with his feet facing in the opposite direction. Taking advantage of the fact that I was watching Joey, Félix took my face in his hands as he had outside the restaurant and kissed me on the mouth. Before I could protest, he was gone, leaving me with stinging lips and a slip of paper on which was a drawing of a Floribunda rose. I put it in the bin.

Because it was Sunday and Jordan was on a break now that Rochelle Eléctronique had got to the contract stage, he came with us to the airport. Although I was the better driver and spent my life in the car — years of shuttling back and forth to the museum and doing the school run, and in Paris circumventing the narrow streets like a cab driver — I sat in the back between my mother and Walter and let him drive.

I had been driving since I was seventeen and had never had an accident (although once my foot had slipped and I had accelerated into the wall of an under-ground parking lot, which Jordan never let me

134

forget), but every time I took the wheel, if Jordan was in the passenger seat, I felt as if I was taking my drivers' test. My automatic pilot, in which mode I could drive and plan dinner, drive and make notes on the memo pad I kept beside me in the car, drive and consult my diary, drive and tune the radio, drive and select a track on a favourite CD, deserted me. It was not that he said anything, except the occasional 'take it easy honey' or 'careful' or 'didn't you notice that guy turning right?' but the fact that his face became more alert than if he were behind the wheel himself, and I could sense him looking right and left at crossroads and glancing in the mirror and even putting his foot on an imaginary brake.

My mother was taking everything out of her purse and checking the passports and tickets for the umpteenth time — she always got nervous when she travelled — when turning round from the front seat where he was sitting next to Jordan, Joey said, 'Who was that man in the park, Mom?'

If Jordan had not been hooting at a dilatory driver and my mother not enquiring of Walter if he was sure that he had all his pills, I might have been in trouble. As it was, Joey, who was tense with excitement at the thought of the flies he was going to tie and the salmon he was going to land, did not wait for an answer.

'Did you pack my Game Boy?'

Wondering if Joey had actually seen Félix kissing me as he executed his Ollie Airwalk, I breathed a sigh of relief and assured him that the Game Boy was in his backpack.

Saying goodbye to Joey, even though it was only for three weeks, did something to my inner being. While my bond with Michelle was undeniable, my feelings for Joey, a mother's for her son, went deeper and were unfathomable. Watching his eager face as, wearing his Red Sox jersey, he clutched his skateboard with its Santa Cruz wheels and jumped up and down like a yoyo between my mother and Walter aiming imaginary karate-chops at some make-believe opponent, I knew I was going to miss him.

I hugged my mother, who with the perception that had stood her in good stead throughout her years as a sales rep told me I was not to worry about Joey, kissed Walter whose smooth cheek smelled of pungent after-shave, and watched Joey hurl himself into his father's arms. When it was my turn I shed a little tear, which I hoped he wouldn't notice as he flung his firm arms round my neck, and watched as he shuffled backwards into the departures, and towards the X-ray machine.

When we got home there was a cellophane-wrapped bouquet of long-stemmed red roses on the console in the hallway. Helga had taken it in.

'They must be for Michelle.' Jordan picked up the bouquet, the scarlet ribbons trailing. 'A secret admirer. There's no card.'

11

If I hadn't gone back to the Musée d'Orsay, that might have been that, but with Michelle and Joey away, Lauren preoccupied with her next collection — autumn was going to see black as the new black — and Jordan, who was busy nailing the deal to the wall, more preoccupied than ever, I was at a loose end.

When I got to the museum I found Félix, who had parked his Kawasaki, sitting on the parapet by the river waiting for me, and I guessed that he must have followed me from the Boulevard Courcelles.

'There's something I'd like to show you.'

When he pursued me into the museum I did not protest. Although my head was doing battle with my heart, I ignored the conflict and part of me even welcomed the company.

Walking around the cool of the Musée d'Orsay with Félix, I had the feeling that, although I was not alone, I was accompanying myself, and despite the fact that neither of us spoke — I was not going to make it easy for him — a dialogue was actually taking place.

Dwarfed by the great arches, we mingled

with the crowds amongst the plasters and bronzes, veering off into the side rooms and stopping, as if in response to a signal, for long moments at a time before a Delacroix or an Ingres, before resuming our itinerary. Passing quickly through the Opéra room with its exhibition of drawings, engravings and photographs, we rode the escalator to the second floor. Wondering what it could possibly be that Félix wanted to show me, I followed him past the Neo-Impressionists, the Pont-Aven School, and the Bonnards and the Vuillards of the Nabis. He stopped suddenly, a look of adulation on his face, before the portrait of the *Lady with a Glove* by Madame Carolus-Duran, a fashionable artist of the late 1860s who painted idealized images of the bourgeoisie. The *Lady with a Glove* was, like Félix, dressed entirely in black — black seemed to hold a fascination for him — from her tiered lace dress with its tiny waist, to the matching black hat, relieved by a yellow rose perched upon black, corkscrew curls. More seductively than any nude, she posed against a background of grey on grey. As she removed her second ivory glove (the first was already flung down, like a gauntlet, on the floor) her eyebrows were arched coquettishly and her dainty little finger was extended. I did not need to ask why he had stopped before the painting. Although the *Lady with the Glove* could not have been more than eighteen, the configuration of the face, and the expression on it, bore more than a passing resemblance to my own.

'It might have started off as a wager,' Félix said, looking at the painting, 'but I would never have gone ahead with it. I'm not a complete shit. I'd like you to understand.'

He touched my elbow, stroking it, scorching the flesh, and with a final glance at the *Lady with a Glove*, as if he was reluctant to leave her, led me towards the escalator. As the dust danced in the sunbeams, I ignored the still small voice that warned me that if I went back again to the rue Dauphine I was undone.

★   ★   ★

We sat at Félix's table beneath the open window. He tried to tell me again, clumsily, that while the outrageous idea of seducing me had been Alexandre's, what started off as a dare, a young man's challenge, had rebounded.

'The object of a wager!' I said. 'How do you think that makes me feel?'

The fact that I had crossed the Pont Neuf on the back of the Kawasaki gave the lie to

140

my indignation. Félix's black linen shirt was open at the neck and desire hovered in the torpid air between us as the hubbub rose from the street below.

'It was unforgivable.'

We did not drink the coffee Félix had made. What had started off as wary conversation became a sequence of orchestrated movements as we first touched finger-tips, then hands, then mouths, until, abandoning the safety of the table, we moved urgently and in tandem towards Félix's bed where we reached the point of no return. After the rush of sex, the high of passion was over and I examined my face in the looking-glass in the bathroom to see if I had grown horns, if anyone could tell. Coming up behind me, Félix caressed my neck then, removing the combs which secured my hair, brushed it slowly, as if time had been arrested, and we spent what was left of the morning in an unhurried replay of mutual possession, shamelessly imbibing and assimilating each other's soul and flesh. Later, as if in gratitude, he kissed my fingers in the place where the candle had burned them and I knew that, like God's rainbow, it was a sign between us. I was at a loss to comprehend the sexual upheaval that consumed me. What I felt for this young man was so new, so sweet, that it did not bear critical examination. I had no desire to go home.

When he dropped me off at the Boulevard Courcelles, I felt a sudden resurgence of the energy that had deserted me for the duration of my Paris sojourn and, despite the fact that the sun was at its zenith, an overwhelming sensation of well-being. The self-satisfied smile was wiped off my face when I put my key into the front door and opened it to find Jordan, dressed for golf, and Sherman, standing in the hallway. Their eyes went to my swollen mouth and tumbled hair as, in a gesture of guilt — there was no way Jordan should have been home so early — I fastened the top button of my dress.

'Lafarge has invited us to play a celebratory round at Fontainebleau.' Jordan's voice was calm. 'Where on earth have you been?'

I put a hand to my cheek.

'I've been to the dentist.' It was my first lie.

I have never used cocaine, never been near a drug and was at a loss to understand what was happening to me, a happily married woman, pierced to the quick by Eros — not Agape or Caritas with their emotions directed towards God or family or friends — whose arrow I could not have pulled from my flesh even had I wanted to. I don't know if the mysteries of attraction have ever been fully explained, nor did I want them to be. There are chemical forces beyond our knowledge and electrical fields which remain uncharted. No one has explained exactly what it is that passes between two strangers across a crowded room; that stops two people in their tracks and fills them with an iron resolve, no matter what the consequences, to meet again. The only trigger powerful enough to ignite the full blaze is the buried, unconscious experience which lies at the heart of each person's love map. I had no desire to explore mine nor to interpret the complex possibilities of sight, sound, scent, suggestion, and memory which had unhinged the nuts and bolts of reason which — since the night of Michelle's birthday party — had fallen into rattling disarray.

With Michelle and Joey away, I had intended to catch up with my reading and correspondence, make plans for returning to Boston, weed out the dross from Joey's wardrobe (he was growing so fast), spend quality time in the Louvre — which over the years had served as prison, arsenal, mint, granary, telegraph station, fort, hotel for visiting heads of state and shopping arcade — and pick up a few bargains in the sales. As with the best-laid plans I did none of these things, but spent every available moment with my lover, whose youth and ardour invoked not only deep erotic responses, but feelings of exhilaration and excitement, the existence of which I had all but forgotten. The only way to escape them was to run, and the reason I did not was because I appeared to have lost the use of my legs.

Félix showed me a Paris in which you could have Degas for breakfast, langoustines for dinner, and Descartes round the clock; a city which, even with the help of Lauren and my guidebooks I would never have discovered for myself.

As, despite the summer egress, car drivers were forced into frayed-tempered immobility, we weaved our way between the stationary traffic on the Kawasaki, or arm-in-arm — I was unlikely to meet anyone I knew — strolled brazenly beneath the plane trees and chestnuts erupting from their metal grates along the August streets. Scattering the pigeons, pausing to read the headlines at the newspaper kiosks, or now and then resting on a bench, our heads close, we left the broad Avenues of Baron Haussmann, the historic monuments to Napoleon, and sought out the exotic quartiers, far removed from the grand hotels and smart restaurants, which multi-ethnic immigrants had made their own.

Eschewing art for literature, we found a

respite from the heat among the vines and wisteria in the hidden garden of a Pigalle mansion filled with the memorabilia of George Sand, Turgenev and Dickens who had once frequented what was now a little known shrine. In a crepuscular and time-defying restaurant, a stone's throw from Félix's studio, where neither the wallpaper, the long black aprons of the waiters, the impeccable service, nor the menu made any concession to modernity, we dined amid the faded prints and antique mirrors on duck of a thousand olives and refreshed our palates with decorative glasses of old-fashioned strawberry ice-cream. At the Village Voice we stumbled upon a poetry reading and I came away, at Félix's insistence, with a leather-bound edition of Elizabeth Barrett Browning's *Sonnets from the Portuguese.*

At home in his studio we did not always make love. Sometimes I watched him paint, absorbed and remote, as we listened to music: Mozart for his joyous celebration of sexuality and love as the storm clouds of revolution gathered in France; Beethoven for grandeur and transcendence; and Wagner when we were feeling sad. Sometimes I arrived to find my serious young man listening to jazz: Tubby Hayes, Ronnie Scott, Miles Davis and Phil Bates. Putting down his palette and holding his brush between his teeth he would gather me up and we would dance to the Beach Boys and The Beatles, *Cheek to Cheek* and *Sketches of Spain*.

One afternoon, strap-hanging to the accompaniment of a Juillard quartet, we took the métro to the cemetery of Père Lachaise. Progressing smoothly from Odéon to Réamur Sebastopol, Réamur Sebastopol to République and République to Père Lachaise, Félix filled me in on the history of the Paris métro — to build which two thousand *oeuvriers* had worked for seventeen months, negotiating 150 kilometres of sewers and ripping out the city's entrails to install new track — with its art nouveau entrances and romantic lines: Abbesses (Line 12), in memory of the Abbaye des Dames de Montmartre, a religious community founded in 1155; Kleber (Line 6), commemorating Jean-Baptiste Kleber, commander of the French Army in Egypt where he met his death in 1800; Rambuteau (Line 12), *préfet de la Seine* from 1833 until 1848, who set in motion plans for the modernization of Paris by installing gas-fuelled street lamps, building pavements, creating squares and improving the city's water supply; Télégraphe (Line 11), one of the deepest in the network, running 20 metres below ground, after engineer Claude

Chappe who experimented with a new telegraph system; and Wagram (Line 3), a village near Vienna where Napoleon I defeated Archduke Charles in 1809.

A similar journey would have seen Jordan, concerned only in getting from A to B in the shortest possible time, with his nose in a newspaper, and the colourful platforms, with their fibreglass seats and unique art work, would have passed him by. At Père Lachaise, Félix generously rewarded the musical quartet who had entertained us on our journey and, as the doors of the train slid open, put a proprietorial arm around my waist.

There are certain times, certain occasions, which stand out in memory; markers — like the breakfast, lunch and dinner of a normal day — which are imprinted upon the longest day of all which is life. Mine, I suppose, are my graduation — my mother had worked incredibly hard to send me to school and was so proud of me — my wedding day, and giving birth for the first time, as well as lesser events, not all of them happy; my father's death, although I did not actually see him slip away; my near fatal attack of peritonitis; watching the sun rise over the Grand Canyon; standing before Tintoretto's *Ascension of the Virgin*; my first date. I added the afternoon at Pére Lachaise with Félix to the collection, threading it on to the necklace of memory like a cool glass bead.

I knew of course, that the famous names buried beneath the trees in the largest park in Paris, read like the pages of *Who's Who* in France, and that there would be monuments and tombstones and family vaults. The surprise — as always when you take the trouble to find out for yourself rather than relying upon received ideas — was that the seats beneath the shady trees were used as picnic tables and children played hide-and-seek uninhibitedly among the graves.

> Passants! Priez pour nous.
> Nous avons été ce que vous
> êtes, et vous serez un jour
> ce que nous sommes.

Putting his arms around me, Félix translated: 'Pray for us. We were once as you are now, and one day you will be as we are.'

I shivered and he held me close.

A black cat, darting out of the shadows, accompanied us up the steep incline to the winding paths which circumvented the last resting-places of celebrated lovers, artists, composers and men of letters. We skirted the monuments and markers, many of which had fallen into desuetude — Frédéric Chopin,

Edith Piaf — and the catafalques of Marcel Proust and Oscar Wilde, born sadly before his time. Memories were perpetuated by flowers and photographs, as if the senses of the dead still lived, as if they could still see; victims of famine and disease, asassination and insurrection, lay marked by carved likenesses, in marble or in stone, expressing with their cold symbolism a profound desire to comprehend the meaning of human existence, perpetuating the ultimate hope that the universe is not random, emphasising the frailty of the human condition, its terror of the unknown.

Félix, who was still young, saw the cemetery as a place of optimism where life everlasting took precedence over death, loss, and mortality, and the sensuous figures of memorial art proclaimed tribute and hope. These surrogate mourners, forever present, forever young, with their alabaster skin, their chipped noses, their voluptuous bodies, their classical drapery, their angels' wings, stood eternal vigil over the 70,000 dead, depicting how great the loss, how deeply missed the deceased. Their images — desecrated by birds, despoiled by the elements — of perfect physical beauty undiminished by time, signified the imposition of order upon the caprices of nature, symbolized the nobility of the human spirit; Death seizing a maiden by the hair and preparing her to descend into the tomb dug at her feet; Death passionately embraced by a young girl; Death with a bow and arrow, arms outstretched in triumph, humanity vanquished; the dead of the Great Plague; the dead of the Holocaust. The vast cemetery, with its 44 hectares, held death in every guise yet, paradoxically, although the sun was blotted out by the unkempt branches of the overhanging trees, none of it seemed sad.

Unwilling to relinquish the thoughts engendered by what should have been, but for some inexplicable reason was not, a macabre afternoon, we stopped in the Place de l'Opéra for a drink. Made newly aware of the preciousness of time by what we had just witnessed, we were reluctant to go home.

We were deep in debate about the merits of the 'art' and, in particular, the bond between sexuality and death which was used as a moralistic pretext to depict female nudity in the context of the cemetery, when a familiar voice said:

'Judith!'

Lauren, halted in mid-flight from the interior of the Café de la Paix, did a double take.

'Judith.'

Although she repeated my name she was staring at Félix.

'Félix Dumoulin . . . ' I introduced my companion who leapt to his feet and shook Lauren's outstretched hand. 'A friend of Michelle's.'

Kissing me on both cheeks, Lauren looked at her watch.

'*Il faut que je m'en aille . . .* '

I saw that she had a taxi waiting at the kerb.

'I'm due in a meeting. I've got to dash.'

As the taxi drove away, I saw Lauren looking towards our table through the back window of the cab. Her mouth hung open in disbelief.

12

We were in the sauna at Le Studio, lying motionless on the wooden slats, our eyes closed.

'A friend of Michelle's!' Lauren said sceptically, getting up to pour more water on the coals. 'You were incandescent. Almost a fire hazard. Where did you find him? How long has it been going on?'

I kept my eyes shut as I debated what to do about Lauren. There was not much choice.

'If Jordan found out he'd kill me. Correction. He'd kill Félix.' Lauren snorted dismissively.

'Everyone in Paris has a *cinq à sept*. Everyone has a *copain* . . . '

'It's not like that.'

'*Bof*!' Lauren was lying down again.

Despite all the time I had spent in Paris I was still not absolutely sure what *bof* meant.

'By the way,' I said, 'I'm having dinner with you tonight.'

'Not tonight, *chérie*,' Lauren slapped her ample thighs. 'Tonight is my 'nothing to eat after 5 o'clock' night.'

'Félix wants to take me to the Train Bleu.'

Realizing that I was asking for an alibi, Lauren was quick off the mark.

'Ah, *dinner*! No problem. I'll deal with Jordan — ' she made herself comfortable on her towel — 'if you tell me about your toy boy.'

Starting with Michelle's birthday party and ending with the afternoon at Père Lachaise and the Café de la Paix where Lauren had discovered us, I told her everything that had happened. In answer to her question — Lauren was always concerned with practicalities — as to how Félix managed to live in a substantial studio in the rue Dauphine with no visible means of support, I explained about his family. His mother had died after a riding accident when he was three, and his father, himself an artist, who had married into the French aristocracy, had remarried and lived in Barbados. Félix had been brought up by his maternal grandparents in a château in the Pas de Calais, which he would one day inherit. On his grandfather's death, his grandmother had gone to live with her only relative, a younger sister in Mulhouse, who had subsequently suffered a stroke and died. His grandmother, whose health was poor and who was unable to live on her own, now resided in an elegant *maison de retraite* in the country, where she looked forward to her grandson's frequent visits. Having been bequeathed an income from his grandfather, Félix was financially independent and could devote himself to his painting. His *oeuvre* had been taken on by a gallery in the Avenue Montaigne and he was beginning to make a name for himself.

'He's already had several exhibitions. Frankfurt, Zurich . . . '

'Good for him. But what's the big attraction?'

I knew exactly what she meant and tried to analyse it, tried to diagnose the strange illness, the unknown drug I had unwittingly swallowed, which had rocked my life to its foundations, affected my neural circuits, and was already beginning to consume me. If it was my hormones which were responsible they had taken me to places outside my control, they had travelled through my blood and I did not want to know. I had no desire to have my actions explained, anatomized, biologized. What I felt for Félix was not so much chemistry as alchemy, a sorcerer's trick. He made me laugh. Sometimes the bed creaked with laughter. He gave me confidence. He reinvented me. In his presence I was endowed with qualities I was unaware I lacked. The levels on which we talked were deep and uninhibited. He was my sounding-board and I his. Schooled by his grandmother who even in her eighties and confined to a retirement home was *impeccable*, Félix understood women, knew what made them tick. He was a time person. Unlike Jordan to whom every moment that passed was a commodity to be accounted for on a balance sheet, Félix used time — whether he was brushing my hair, slowly, sensuously, or engrossed in the preliminaries of love — as if it were infinite.

I was willing to impart none of this to Lauren, nor to confess that when Félix and I were not together I was feverish with longing, tormented by the need to see him, to hear his voice, weak with uncontrollable desire.

'Get real, Judith . . . ' Lauren said.

I was sorry I had said so much about Félix. I could have made up some story about our presence in the café to put Lauren off the scent. She was making me angry.

' . . . The guy is twenty-eight years old. He sees you as his mother.'

I sat up, feeling as if I might burst and needing the plunge pool. The heat of my body was not engendered entirely by the sauna.

'Don't be ridiculous.' Standing up I put my towel around my waist.

'I love you, Judith. I'm speaking to you as a friend. No good can come of it.'

'You're a fine one to talk.'

'Okay, okay. I have my *équipe*, my captains of industry, my publishers, my ski instructors, my tennis coaches . . . I've never made any secret of it. I need variety. It's like steak au poivre.'

'Steak au poivre?'

'I adore steak au poivre, but I wouldn't want to eat it every day of the week. It's different for me, Judith,' Lauren's voice became serious. 'I don't have a Jordan. I don't have a Michelle. I don't have a Joey. All I have is a whole bunch of patterns for the spring collection, a whole pile of order books. I'd throw the lot in the garbage if the right man came along.'

I got home from Le Train Bleu at midnight to find Jordan looking worried. There was no need to invoke Lauren with her 'nothing to eat after 5 o'clock' as my alibi. He had only just got in and did not ask. There was a postcard on the table from Joey with a picture of the quaint fishing lodge where they were staying, the excited news that he had caught a six-pound grilse with a fly which he had tied himself, a row of hugs and kisses, and a PS to Helga reminding her to feed his tropical fish.

'There's some cold cuts in the fridge.'

My lover and I, côté à côté on the banquette at Le Train Bleu, had eaten Foie

Gras Frais de Canard washed down with a glass of Château Grand Péyruchet 1987; Coquilles St Jacques Fraîches à la Provençale; Côtes de Veau Laitier aux Pâtes Fraîches; Fromage Fermier au Lait Cru de Brébis du Parc 'Livradois-Forez'. We drank two bottles of Beaune 'Clos de la Chaume', and made love to each other beneath the long table with its copious white cloth.

'I had dinner with Sherman.'

Don't do that, Félix, I will die.

'Is something the matter?'

I love you Judith.

'I sincerely hope not . . . '

No.

'Claude rang me today . . . '

Félix, please!

'He's setting up a meeting — '

Embrasse-moi.

' — with a senior civil servant from the Foreign Office . . .

There.

Encore.

'The Viscomte de Loisy.'

We had left the restaurant after the cheese. Not waited for coffee. In an alley near the Gare de Lyon we finished what we had begun. A putain and her John. It was not yet dark.

'The Viscomte de Loisy. What does he want?'

'I don't know.'

'You'll soon find out.'

The Rochelle Eléctronique deal had taken over his life and had cost more than $20 million. I tried to be reassuring.

'Not until Thursday . . . '

Today was Tuesday.

'Claude's in Montecatini.'

Jordan took me in his arms and I tried not to pull away, terrified lest he detect Félix on my summer skirt.

'I've been neglecting you lately. I'll tell you what. Why don't we take a drive out, tomorrow. There's nothing I can do until Thursday. We'll have lunch on the river.'

Afterwards, like two young lovers, we walked the streets of Paris, stopping to watch a disdainful model in a ballgown, pose for a shoot outside an old pissoire. Félix had his arm around me.

'' . . . *Paris, joli Paris, qu'un jour dut crée l'amour* . . . '

Spend the night with me, Judith.

He was insane.

★   ★   ★

The day on which Jordan was to take me to the river dawned as enervating as the others. I had promised Félix we would go to the Jeu de

Paume and, while Jordan wrapped up a few things at the bank, I called to tell him that I was not going to make it. He sounded upset, tried to persuade me to make some excuse to Jordan, to tell him I was otherwise engaged.

'I'll come this evening. When we get back . . . ' I reckoned that Jordan would be busy.

'Promise?'

'*Je promets.*'

I would rather have gone to the Jeu de Paume than spend the day in the country with Jordan and wanted to ride the magic carpet that would take me there. I tried to ignore the 'folly of the mind' that possessed me, to douse the unquenchable fire, to forget the agreeable illness with which I was consumed and — for the duration of the day at least — to be a good wife. It was not because, as a husband, Jordan did not satisfy me that I had taken a lover. Not the typical unhappily married woman cheating on her husband. I knew that every marriage was a journey, that partners mutate, and that the couple who set out together are not the same two people after eighteen years. We had learned the hard way that marriage is rarely the undiluted wedded bliss of poetry and fiction and our relationship — a reproduction of Lavoisier's portrait of a loving husband

and wife hung in the bedroom of our Boston home — was based on a profound shared connection. Looking at the current statistics on long-term marriages such as ours, I did not envy the women of today the pain of divorce, the child abuse implicit in splitting up, the hardship of single-parenthood, the straitened circumstances in which many were forced to live. While it was no longer necessary for a wife to submerge her identity in that of her husband, it did not seem sensible to me for women to give up on wifehood. That was what I told Michelle.

Driving out of Paris with Jordan as he sang, tunelessly, " . . . It's a bright sunny day in the meadow. It's a bright sunny day in the sky. The grass is as high as an elephant's eye, and I think I am falling in love . . . " As he negotiated the traffic and held my hand simultaneously, I wondered, but not for long, why Judith Flatland, in her smart linen trouser suit, was present in the passenger seat of the limo, while her mind was elsewhere.

The restaurant, which had a Michelin rosette, had been recommended by one of Jordan's colleagues at Offenbach Frères. It was by the waterside on a bend in the river and on the bank the tables, prettily bedecked with pink cloths and napery, were set out beneath matching umbrellas at the water's edge. The mouth-watering buffet, from which guests helped themselves, carrying their plates over the tufted grass, was in a farmhouse set back from the road. The setting was romantic, Jordan was in good spirits, my cream suit flattered me, and the day, a real *fête champêtre* despite the marauding wasps, should have been idyllic.

'Won't be long now,' Jordan raised his glass, Blanc de Blancs to cool the day in which there was no cloud.

Raising my own glass I saw Félix's face imposed on Jordan's as he smiled:

'To Filene's Basement.'

Filene's Basement. Married Esperanto. Filene's Basement in Boston tagged each sale item with the date of arrival and a marked-down price which was mercilessly reduced, week by week, until any goods which remained were donated to charity. Filene's Basement, where the ladies of Boston moved in human waves through the tables of close-out articles from other stores. It was a family joke and whenever I had a new jacket or a pair of pants or had bought something extravagant for Michelle and shirked confessing the price to Jordan, we'd tell him we had bought it in Filene's Basement.

'Like old times,' Jordan leaned forward to kiss me across the table.

'Like old times.'

His eyes lingered on my face.

'You should always wear your hair that way.'

I had appropriated one of Michelle's Alice Bands and, at Félix's insistence, now wore my hair loose.

'Paris agrees with you.'

'You think so?'

'You could be eighteen.'

Terrified lest he read something in my face, I said:

'It's the Blanc de Blancs . . . ' and pointed to the bottle we had emptied between us.

'It's the truth . . . ' Jordan put his napkin on the table. 'They say the desserts are out of this world.'

We climbed up the gentle incline of the bank, the three-inch heels of my sandals piercing the earth. All around us happy couples were intent on conversation, family parties laughing and making a great deal of noise.

Madame la Patronne, sharp eyes everywhere, stamped from a familiar French mould soon to fall into desuetude, took Jordan under her wing.

'Mousse au chocolat, mousse aux framboises . . . '

'Did you make them?'

Seduced by his charm and shaking her head coquettishly, Madame smiled at Jordan revealing her gold teeth.

' . . . Îles Flottantes, Bavarois Vanille, *fraises* Chantilly, Tarte Tatin . . . '

He cut short the litany.

'Give me some of that apple pie.'

There was no dithering for Jordan, no hovering, no second glance. He stood with his plate, poised by the door, while I made up my mind.

'You know darling,' he said when I had put my spoon down on the mousse au chocolat. 'When this deal is all done and dusted, I think we should have a farewell dinner at the apartment. Lafarge, Sherman, Powers, Farell, the whole team . . . '

He saw my look of horror.

'I want you to hire the best caterer in Paris. Why don't you have a word with Nadine?'

13

In the event we didn't finish lunch until 4.30 and by the time we reached the Boulevard Courcelles it was too late for Jordan to do anything useful at the bank. There was no way I could go to the rue Dauphine. I did not even dare telephone Félix. Determined to devote himself to me, and to take his mind off his forthcoming meeting with the Viscomte de Loisy, Jordan proposed a game of Scrabble. Going along with his suggestion, but with my mind elsewhere, I scored a lousy one hundred and fifty points to his four hundred before he got busy with his memo-recorder leaving me to fix something to eat. After we'd had supper, although neither of us was very hungry, Jordan, who had been growing increasingly amorous — a state of affairs which I had done my best to ignore — wanted to make love. Pleading a headache, the heat and the effects of the Blanc de Blancs we had drunk at lunch, I suggested, as tactfully as I could, a deferment to another time. When he had got over his disappointment, and was trying to put a brave face on what he had clearly intended as a grand finale to a perfect day, he took me in his arms.

'Are you sure you're okay, darling? Your mother was worried about you.'

'I'm fine.' I wondered what Félix was doing.

'Why don't *you* go down to the villa? It would do you good.'

I was brushing my hair in front of the mirror and did not reply. On the dressing-table, crowded in their silver frames, were the family photos, our *lares* and *penates* marking the happy high points in our lives. Jordan and me laughing ecstatically, our arms around each other on our honeymoon; Michelle when she was one day old; the Flatland family on horseback (we had spent our summer vacation on a ranch); all of us, complete with dog and the hamster Joey was holding up to the camera, in our backyard.

In the looking-glass, I could see Jordan who was carrying out his bedtime ritual, meticulously placing his watch, his mobile phones, his memo-recorder and his electronic organizer in absolute symmetry on the Boulle commode. I was aware that this quest for perfection inherited directly from his mother, led him to be a leader in his field, but occasionally, when, in the time it takes most people to blink, he insisted on putting things away before I had finished with them, or checking, straightening, and rearranging anything he found 'positionally wrong', it drove me to distraction. Lauren said I didn't know when I was well off. That living with a man who was obsessionally tidy was a great deal better than sharing with a slob who never cleaned up after himself and created a one-man rubbish tip around him each time he sat on the sofa. Knowing how Lauren felt about Jordan, she would, of course, say that.

Next morning, when Jordan, clearly apprehensive about his deal, had left for his meeting with Lafarge and the mysterious Viscomte de Loisy, I telephoned Félix. Getting no reply, I guessed that he had gone out for his *petit déjeuner* and set out for the rue Dauphine.

I loved Paris, any city, in the early morning when its face was being washed and it was making animated preparations for what the new day would bring. In the rue de Buci, the gutters were running with water, the pavements in front of the shops were being swept and the shutters raised. Too early for tourists, the indigent population strolled with their croissants and their newspapers, their dogs and their baguettes, dodging the coursing rivulets and negotiating their way among the crates of fresh flowers, among the café tables which, with their bowls of sugar-cubes and *demi-tasses*, overflowed on to the sidewalk. I looked for Félix in Paul, where two dusty young chefs rolled dough in the plate-glass window and the waitress knew him and usually had his *grand café* and his *demi-flûte* ready. She nodded in recognition then shook her head. He was not in the *tabac*, with its window display of fluorescent rulers, pencil-cases and highlighters ready for the return to school, nor was he in the *traiteur* with its daily offerings of Jambon Maison, Riz à la Tomate and Artichauts Cuits scrawled illegibly on its blackboard.

Making my way to the rue Dauphine past the ethnic goods emporium which sold scarves and beaded bags of orange and burnt sienna, I punched the code on his door and climbed the steep stairs to the fourth floor.

'Félix . . . It's me.'

The painting of Olympe on the easel had given way to two figures, tentatively outlined, on a bench beneath a lilac tree, and I recognized the gravelled garden of the Musée de la Vie Romantique. There were clothes everywhere; Félix's black shirt, his shoes. The door to his bedroom was open and he lay spreadeagled on his low mattress deep in innocent sleep. I was creeping towards his comatose form, thinking to surprise him, when I noticed two empty wine glasses on the floor beside the rumpled bed, and in the ashtray the remains of two joints.

Not wanting to think what I was thinking, I returned to the studio. On the table were a pair of ox-blood earrings, a spent book of matches from a club much favoured by the *jeunesse dorée*, two plates, and the remains of what looked like a hastily eaten supper.

It was no more than I deserved for dismissing the fact that I was the result of a wager, the object of a young man's fantasy, for making myself a middle-aged fool. I stared out of the open window at the terracotta view that had once thrilled me, transported me to forbidden pastures, quickened my racing heart. The mother in me pulled down the blind on the rising sun lest it damage the painting. I wondered should I leave a note.

'Judith.'

His voice stopped me in the tracks I was making for the door. I did not reply.

'Judith . . . ' He sounded frightened. 'Wait! I can explain.'

No explanation was necessary. Halfway across the room, I could not have moved had I wanted to. I was already drowning. Already a lost soul.

When I did not turn up the previous evening as promised, Félix had been unable to work, unable to concentrate. Desperate for company he had called Olympe. An exchange of confidences — Olympe had a new man in her life — had led to a get-together with Alexandre and Nicolas, with Laurent and Natasha, with Kiki and Juliette . . . '

'Like old times . . . ' Echoing Jordan I interrupted the explanation which came from the bedroom and with which Félix attempted to delay me.

'I haven't been clubbing since I met you.'

Did he think I did not belong in the youthful milieux they frequented? Was he ashamed of me in front of his friends?

He came to stand beside me, naked and dazed with sleep. I picked up the earrings from the table and placed them in his outstretched hand.

'Olympe?' I recognized them from his painting of her.

He made no attempt to deny it. 'Forgive me. It won't happen again. I was angry. I was not myself.'

Aristotle was wrong when he declared man to be a rational animal, and Pascal right when he assigned much of our behaviour to the antics of the human heart. While I was clearly directed by the activity of my brain which was giving me a clear message, I was the victim of my instinct, of my self-serving desires and, fully aware of the chance I was taking, I did nothing, could do nothing, to minimize the risk.

I did not even listen to the ongoing saga of how it had come about that Olympe had spent the night, and paid little attention to the ardent protestations with which Félix lured me into the same bed where the passion and the exultation he aroused in me proved shamingly undiminished.

By way of compensation for his betrayal, he insisted on taking me to the Eiffel Tower. Disgorged from the packed elevator we stood among the sightseers with their binoculars, circumventing the windy platform like a couple of kids out of school. Holding on to my wind-swept hair and my wrap-over skirt which was rapidly becoming unwrapped, I followed Félix's extended finger as he pointed out the sights:

'Bois de Boulogne . . . La Défense . . . '

I didn't know why I had agreed to climb the tower with him. I was scared of heights.

' . . . Bois de Vincennes, Orly . . . '

'Félix, let's go.'

Buffeted by the gale, afraid to look down, to look in front of me, I hid my face in my hands. It couldn't have been for more than a moment, but when I raised my head Félix had gone.

'Félix . . . '

Swaying, I hung on to the railings, surrounded by a press of strangers, too weak to move on my own.

'Félix! Félix!'

Among the miscellany of faces not a single one was familiar, there was no one who could help me, no one whom I knew. I thought I was going to faint, that I would fall over the side into nothingness, although I knew that was impossible and that the first thing I must do was to move out of the savagery of the wind. I fought my way to the sanctuary of the gift shop where Félix, oblivious to my panic attack, was calmly making a purchase, and threw myself into his surprised arms.

'That wasn't funny,' I said, when I had calmed down.

Stroking my hair reassuringly and holding me close, he looked into my eyes.

'*This* isn't funny.'

I knew what he meant.

Elbowing our way through the crowds into the next available car — I was not going to stay on the platform one moment longer than was necessary — we stood shored up by the press of bodies amidst the Babel of tongues, watching the ground below approach.

'I'm afraid.' The remark was intended for Félix's ears alone.

A German with a camera smiled understandingly.

'Is better you don't look, Madame.'

He wasn't to know that my apprehension did not relate to the stomach-churning descent. I buried my face in Félix's shoulder and he held me close.

★　★　★

When Jordan came home I did not need to ask him how his meeting with the Viscomte de Loisy had gone; it was written on his face. It was not until we had finished dinner that the full story came out. It took me some time to piece it together.

The Viscomte de Loisy had inadvisedly kept Jordan waiting in Claude Lafarge's office at the Ministry of Defence (something which Jordan never did). He had turned out to be an extremely arrogant senior civil servant who told Jordan that he had only recently been informed of the proposed aquisition of Rochelle Eléctronique by Cavendish Holdings. The French Foreign Office, whom he represented, was extremely worried in case the American owners of Cavendish Holdings might, at some future date, involve Rochelle Eléctronique in transactions with countries which were hostile to France. To prevent this,

172

they insisted upon retaining the right of veto. This meant, in effect, that although France was in favour of economic expansion and investment by foreign companies, the Foreign Office was not prepared to endanger her standing within the international community.

'I have never heard such bullshit.' Jordan was beside himself. 'What the bastard proposes is that the only way he will allow the Rochelle deal to go ahead as Lafarge has agreed, is if the government retains the golden share.'

'Golden share?'

I was doing my best to understand.

'A share in Rochelle Eléctronique which would enable any decisions and any resolutions passed by the company to be blocked.'

'By whom?'

'By enough new directors — appointed by them of course — to overrule the existing board.'

'I'm not with you.'

'OK. Cavendish Holdings will be the new owners of Rochelle Eléctronique and the shareholders will be paid a very good price, as agreed, for what they are selling. The French Government, however, will retain the power to refuse to allow them to engage in any transaction which it considers a threat to its security.'

'What was your response?'

'I got extremely angry.'

I had rarely seen Jordan angry.

'I pointed out that this would devalue the equity of Rochelle by at least 20 per cent — several hundred million dollars — and that under no circumstances could I proceed with the deal were such a condition to be imposed . . . '

I felt extremely sorry for Jordan who, together with Sherman and many other people both in Paris and Boston, had been working so hard and for so long.

'To bring this up at the last moment, just when contracts are about to be signed, is absolutely outrageous, not to mention immoral! I insisted that the condition be immediately withdrawn.'

By the unfamiliar set of Jordan's face, tense and unapproachable, I guessed that his suggestion had not been well :ived.

'The Viscomte is 'not prepared to take a chance'. He made out that he had not been informed of the predicament until recently, which I very much doubt, and that the position of the French Government is just as he outlined it and is not negotiable.'

Storming out of the meeting, Jordan had gone back to Offenbach Frères where he had discussed the situation with his colleagues.

The general feeling seemed to be that although the Viscomte had played an extremely dirty trick on Jordan, pressure might still be brought to bear and the French Government persuaded to change their minds.

'To spring something like that on us at the last minute . . . They're a bunch of shits.' Jordan punched in a number on his telephone. 'George? I *know* you're in Hyannis Port. I know you're on vacation. It *is* urgent. I'm not concerned about the market right now and I'm even less concerned about your putting. That's the problem. We haven't signed. We've run into a major obstacle. OK. OK. Call me back.'

Jordan swapped his phone for his memo-machine.

''Memo to George Grabfield and Nicholas Alrich — Fitch, Lane, Alrich and Newmark, New York . . . ' Sorry about this darling, but I may have to go back to Boston.'

An idea was already taking shape in my head.

'The situation is serious. It has to be sorted out.'

I put my arms around him, comforting him.

'I guess I'm going to be extremely busy for the next couple of weeks. I'm glad we had our day out.'

14

The villa that Lauren had rented for us was in Cap d'Antibes. Low built, with its feet in the water and with only two bedrooms — one of which Michelle and Joey had to share — it was furnished, down to the last designer hand-towel and teacup, entirely in blue and white. So far, since we had been in Paris, we had managed to visit it only once.

'Are you sure you know what you're doing?' Lauren said, when I told her my plan.

I did not reply. Although the idea had been mine, the catalyst had been Félix. Sunning ourselves outside the Deux Magots, imbued with the aura of de Beauvoir and Sartre, he had, with mock-seriousness, produced a package from his pocket.

'I want you to have this.'

I opened it with trepidation. It was a plastic snow-storm. When I shook it, slow white flakes settled over the Eiffel Tower.

Félix took hold of my wrist.

'Come away with me Judith.'

I smiled, deprecatingly, as to a child who had made a ridiculous suggestion.

'I want to spend the night — the nights — with you.'

The words had reverberated in my head, reaching a crescendo when Jordan had suggested that while he was pulling the chestnuts of his deal out of the conflagration created by the Viscomte de Loisy, *I* should go down to the villa. The following day, as he packed his bag for Boston, I told him, trying to sound casual, that I thought his idea a good one. I did not mention that I did not plan to go to the villa by myself.

'I'll have a word with Sherman . . .' Jordan placed a pile of the sparkling white shirts he habitually wore and which were made to measure, symmetrically into his case. 'Why don't you take Nadine?'

Fortunately Nadine could think of nothing worse than the Côte d'Azur in August. She was terrified of getting bitten by mosquitoes and prone to prickly heat. While Sherman was away she would occupy herself with finding a caterer who was not on his *fermeture annuelle* for the celebration dinner upon which a blight had now been cast, and planning a menu worthy of her talents with which everyone concerned would be pleased.

'Nobody tells me that *I* look tired,' Lauren said. 'That *I* could do with a couple of weeks in Antibes.'

'Will you keep an eye on Jordan?'

'Need you ask!'

Helga, whose culinary repertoire consisted largely of wiener schnitzel, also promised to take care of Jordan, as far as the housekeeping was concerned, when he got back from Boston. As if making provision for Jordan mitigated my effrontery, I filled the newly repaired freezer with his favourite dishes and made my plans.

Jordan, who thought of everything, had had Eunice buy me a ticket — Paris to Nice — open-ended so that I could come home at will. In the event, Félix managed to borrow Alexandre's ancient Merc and we went to the villa by car.

It was a long time since I had travelled any distance with a man in an otherwise empty car. Conditioned by years of stocking up our station-wagon with bags of chips and candy and games and their favourite CDs and cassettes for Michelle and Joey, and rugs and blankets for the dog who hated long journeys, when Félix picked me up outside the Pharmacie de Ville (our trysting place) behind the Boulevard Courcelles and I climbed into the passenger seat I had the distinct impression that I had forgotten something, that something vital was missing. It was, of course. The sound of 'Daddy, are we there yet?' 'Mom, she's squishing me!' Jordan's authoritative voice, 'I'm warning you. Don't make me stop this car!' as for mile after mile of enforced proximity we counted cows and played interminable games of 'I-spy'.

As I made my illicit escape from the diesel fumes of Paris with Félix, I recalled the summer vacation when Joey threw a tantrum in a restaurant; the one when Jordan had to pull in every few miles for Michelle to throw up (she was incubating chicken-pox); and others when, no matter how many times they were cautioned, Michelle and Joey ran into their hotel rooms on arrival and proceeded to jump on the beds. One of the things Jordan did on a long journey was to give the kids a map of the USA so that they could track where we were at any given moment. Whenever we got within ten miles of a state line he'd tell them to start watching for the 'Welcome' sign and the first one to see it would get a prize. If I felt guilty at sitting in the Merc next to Félix, it was paradoxically for not having Joey and Michelle in the back, although, in reality, it was they who had gone away, leaving me in Paris on my own.

Saying goodbye to Jordan, who promised to call me at the villa to say when he'd be back in Paris — hopefully with the Viscomte de Loisy debacle well and truly sorted — I almost lost my nerve. Although I had done nothing else for the past few weeks I was not accustomed to deceiving him. A born organizer, of those around him as well as himself, he made sure I knew how to turn on the water and electricity in the villa — 'be sure everything's shut down when you leave' — to remember to bring the terrace cushions in at night, and not to leave the blinds down when it rained. His paternalism was the price I paid for getting married in my twenties. I wondered would he feel as responsible if he got married again, if he took a second wife . . . Shocked by my own discursive thoughts that I had no desire to pursue, and which seemed not to make much sense, I turned to find Félix gazing at me with a look that stopped my heart.

He put his hand over mine.

'Where were you?'

In the realms of the unimaginable, I did not reply.

Of course, once we had left Paris and were on the autoroute, Félix, twenty-eight years old and not averse to taking chances, drove the Merc too fast. Accustomed to freeways where the speed limit was a sedate 55 miles per hour, my heart was in my mouth as he entered the lists for the rush to the south in the exclusively male battle of *amour propre*. As the kilometres clocked up and we skirted Dijon, Lyon, Valence and Orange, passed fields of sunflowers and meadows of yellow rape, the Boulevard Courcelles receded into the distance and it was not only Paris that I left behind.

Although I had visited the villa in Antibes only once with Jordan, I was not unfamiliar with Provençe. I had spent a week in Aix in my student days, in a room with poor lighting, a brass bedstead, an old-fashioned closet, and a telephone of archaic design, the function of which was mainly symbolic since no amount of jiggling the gibbet on which it was suspended could capture the attention of the *standardiste*. The hotel in the rue Cardinale, although simple and clean, had probably remained unchanged since Cézanne had left his imprint on the red-tiled farmhouses and undulating meadows of the surrounding countryside. When Vincent Van Gogh moved from Paris to Arles, the region, with its celebrated light, had yet to cast its spell upon artists. It soon became the fashion, however, for painters to haunt the narrow streets of le Cannet, Sillans, Tourette, Vence, Mougins and Cagnes, and it was not long before Matisse, Renoir, Chagall and my beloved Picasso made the sun-bleached hamlets, the perched villages, and the olive groves their own. *Tout passe, tout lasse, tout casse.* There were still plenty of good painters in the area but now they were outnumbered by indifferent ones, and Provençe had become a mecca for tawdry craft shops, the conduit for mediocre works.

Arriving at Notre Rêve with Jordan and the children, had been a matter of activating the essential services, unpacking the suitcases, visiting the *supermarché*, filling the fridge — Jordan could not survive long without his cold drinks — restraining Joey and Michelle from plunging straight into the translucent sea. Arriving with Félix, before we had opened the shutters, before we had walked out on to the terrace and gazed at the lights along the foreshore, for it was dark when we arrived, we dropped our few clothes on the blue and white tiles and, falling upon the bed, made ardent love.

What can I say about the two illusory weeks in heat that exhausted and enveloped us? That we swam naked in the shallow water which lapped at the foot of the villa, lunched lengthily beneath vine-covered trellises, dined at cool tables amid fountains and jars of giant gladioli, danced intimately to Piaf and Gainsbourg, listened to candle-lit concerts in cobbled squares, eavesdropped on street musicians, browsed in open-air markets with their *pissaladières* and pots of basil, stepped over prostrate dogs taking refuge from the heat, picnicked beneath umbrella pines among the ants and the beetles and the green leafhoppers, climbed up to fortified towns where geraniums hung from window-sills and geckos darted from cracks in dry stone walls, gorged on berries and peaches, visited the Biennale at Monte Carlo, renewed our acquaintance with Matisse and Chagall at Cimiez, with Léger at Biot, Cocteau at Menton, and Picasso — not far from the rented villa — at Antibes.

When Jordan phoned, to say that he was back in Paris and dining on Helga's wiener schnitzel, that Michelle (who had called from Genoa) had had her credit card stolen, that it was raining in Scotland and Joey had inadvertently sat on a fish-hook which had to be removed by the ghillie, and that George Grabfield was pulling the necessary strings in Boston to persuade the French Government to change its mind about the golden share, it was as if he were in another country, as if he spoke a different language. When he asked me, concerned, whether I was managing, whether I was happy on my own, I crossed my fingers and assured him I was fine.

I was lying topless, my eyes closed against

the early morning sun, on the blue and white striped lounger on our minute patch of sand, when a kiss, light as a butterfly's wings, landed on my shoulder.

We had decided to spend the whole day at the villa to allow Félix to paint, but he was fully dressed — black shirt, black chinos (Félix would not be seen dead in shorts), black espadrilles — and carried a blue and white shopping basket.

'Today is Judith day . . . '

'It's not my birthday.'

'I don't want you to lift a finger. I'll cook lunch. The kitchen is strictly out of bounds.'

He set the table, blue and white tablemats, bubbled blue glasses from Biot, on the terrace amid the oleander and pelargonium. Salade Niçoise with glistening anchovies and shiny black olives, an ambrosial cassoulet rich with pork and with cannelini beans, followed by a plate of Chèvre with sweet Reine Claude greengages. Stupefied by the food and the pastis which had been followed by a bottle of Bandol rosé, we sat, replete, for a long while, each with his thoughts, looking out at the diamanté sea with its sailing boats and the sky innocent of clouds. I was the first to break the silence.

'Jordan doesn't like it when I don't speak. It makes him nervous.'

''*Chaque atome de silence est la chance d'un fruit mûr.*''

More than a little drunk, I raised my empty glass to Félix.

'Congratulations to the cook!'

He looked suitably modest.

'I'll do the dishes. It's only fair.'

Gathering the plates on to the blue and white tray I walked barefoot over the cool tiles to the minuscule kitchen. On every available surface were scattered tinfoil containers of varying sizes and carrier bags bearing the legend *Madame Fave: traiteur*.

'You cheat!' My voice could have been heard in Monaco as I rushed out through the sliding windows on to the terrace where Félix, quick as a flash, eluded my flailing fists and dashed into the sea. 'You've been to Madame Fave!' I splashed in after him. 'You didn't cook a thing.'

Whereas Jordan was a classy swimmer, a skill he had passed on to the children, Félix, who could manage no more than a dog-paddle, never ventured out of his depth. I caught him up in the shallows and attempted to pull him beneath what passed for waves as punishment. Restraining me, he took me in his arms and my anger at his deception subsided.

Standing up to our waists in the ocean,

Félix held me at arms length, the water hanging in droplets from the black hairs on his chest. His face was serious.

'Judith, we have to talk . . . '

I turned my head, away from his steady gaze, away from the burning sun.

'There's something I have to tell you.'

'If it's about Madame Fave, forget it. I'll never forgive you.'

'It's not about Madame Fave. I love you, Judith. I'm not going to let you go.'

I took my breasts, which had fed Michelle, suckled Joey, in my hands. 'I'm old enough . . . '

'Marry me.'

'I'm already married.'

'You do a marriage when you're young, then you find out what you've really been looking for. What makes you happy. What you need.'

'I love Jordan . . . '

'To think you can love only one person for the whole of your life is like expecting a candle to burn for ever. Don't go back to Boston, Judith.'

' . . . I do love Jordan.'

He put a damp hand beneath my chin raising my eyes to his.

'Then why are you here, *les pieds dans l'eau, la main dans la mienne?*'

15

I'm not sure when I first realized that I was in love with Félix and that what had begun as a game, the last bastion of the disenchanted wife, had got out of hand. Some say that love is blind, others that it defies explanation, and the more scientifically minded that lovesickness is merely a specific and clear-cut type of brain activity which could lead otherwise sober-minded people to abandon the security of their lives and give everything up for a stranger. For doctors, since Hippocratic times, lovesickness was not so much about love as about fixation. Its victims, wavelengths coincided in a primeval connection, would find themselves unable to rid themselves of obsessive thoughts about some usually unattainable object, and the cure for the malady was sex.

The question was whether you fall in love with a person because you have great sex, or whether you have great sex because you are in love: is passion created in our synapses or in our souls? In the absence of personal affection, can the condition truly be regarded as love, which is sometimes described as akin to madness and, in its most severe form can drive a lover clinically insane. Looking back now, I could see that what had drawn me towards Félix in the first place was a mixture of exhilaration, pleasure and danger which had evolved into exploration, excitement, care and compassion until finally, and this was something I refused to admit even to myself, it began to bear a suspicious resemblance to love.

Having declared himself to be in love with me while we were at Cap d'Antibes, Félix begged me to admit that his feelings were reciprocated. It was not so simple, and the first ridiculous thing that occurred to me was to ask Jordan, who had for so long been my mentor. I tried to analyse my feelings, to catch the emotions as they went haywire in my head and having snared them to martial them into some sort of order. It was a pointless exercise, like trying to make sense of the ineffable or unravelling an intricate web. I needed Félix every moment of every day, becoming distraught if I could not see him, could not touch him. Without doubt he was my *raison d'être* and I grew frantic if he was not there. As the days went by and the time grew near for me to go back to Jordan, to my life, as attractive as the prospect seemed — I missed my husband, wanted to see my children — I knew that Félix had the keys to part of me I had not known existed and it was a part I did not want to leave. Our relationship was no longer only about the fascination of sex. Sometimes we did not touch each other for hours at a time.

'I am enchanted by your face,' Félix said as we lay on the sunloungers beneath the blue and white striped awning, he on his elbow, consuming me with his eyes. Sometimes his English bordered on the quaint. 'You are my Héléne of Troy, my Mary Queen of Scots, my Emma Hamilton, my Greta Garbo, my Marilyn Monroe . . . I would like to paint you.'

'I'm not a good sitter.' I was too impatient.

'I didn't say I was going to paint you. I said I would like to paint you.'

It was too hot for conundrums. Félix opened the *Sonnets from the Portuguese* which was never far from my side:

" 'I love not for those eyes, nor haire,
Nor cheekes, nor lips, nor teeth so rare;
Nor for thy speech, they necke, nor breast,
Nor for thy belly, nor the rest;
Nor for thy hand, nor foote so small,
But wouldst thou know (deere sweet) for all.' "

There were tears in my eyes. It was not the sun. I recognized the moment and tried to

189

hold it to me, to stop time from passing, to defy what the future might bring. Holding out my arms to my lover we rose as one and walked on our bare feet, embracing, into the cool, into the penumbra of our blue and white house.

Making love with Félix, unlike making love with Jordan — he was far too cautious — was to make love in risky places, to take one's partner for *la danse de la séduction*, the aim being to win them over rather than simply getting them into bed. If love-making for Jordan, while unequivocal and tender, bordered on the prosaic, sleeping with Félix, of which I never tired, entailed touchingly attentive gestures, innovation and diversity, distractions and amusements often *un peu fantasiste*. Perhaps it was because at Cap d'Antibes we had time. Time to talk — with Jordan there was little dialogue — time to explore, time to experiment, time, above all, to laugh.

'You and I could make beautiful children,' Félix murmured in the half-light that filtered through the drawn blinds.

'Don't even think about it.'

A boy, dark like Félix; a girl with his Gallic charm.

'I have two children. Jordan would never let them go.'

'Do we have to talk about Jordan?'

'It's OK for you. You have no one to consider. Nothing to lose . . . '

Stopping the utterances he had no wish to hear with his kisses, Félix put his mind to the task in hand, one which if we so desired could be extended, and often had been, to fill the entire afternoon in which the heat, almost physical in its intensity, seemed to have attained a manic crescendo. We had reached the core of our beings, the acme of our love, when I heard a noise.

'What was that?'

'*Rien.*'

'I heard something, Félix.'

'The *stores* . . . ' the blue and white blinds. 'Probably a mistral.'

Lulled into acceptance I caressed his flesh. His head, with its lustrous dark hair, was sweetly between my thighs when I heard the noise again, soft footfalls. I glanced round in time to see the door to the bedroom pushed open, causing me to freeze. A female form appeared, silhouetted against the light. Blinking with incredulity I recognized my Calvin Klein teeshirt.

'Michelle!'

The *tableau vif* would haunt me to the end of my days. The half-light of the soporific afternoon trapped in the chalk-white room,

191

the bed with its tumbled linen, my daughter's uncomprehending expression of horror, my naked lover. Before we could move, the door slammed shut and there was the sound of sobbing; a wail as for a dead person; a piercing cry of disbelief.

Félix was the first to recover. Getting out of bed, he touched my shoulder reassuringly. I retrieved my robe from the bathroom and motioned him not to accompany me, to let me deal with Michelle. Neither of us spoke.

She was curled up on the capacious chair in the salon, howling into a blue cushion. I stretched out my hand.

'Don't touch me!' The sound was that of an animal in pain. 'You're disgusting. I'll never speak to you again!'

I wondered how Michelle had got there, what she was doing on the Cap when the last week of her vacation was to be spent living it up in Juan les Pins. Later I discovered that whilst they were in Genoa, Lois had had to go home because her mother was ill and Jordan had suggested to Michelle that before going on to Juan, she should look in on me at the villa to make sure that I was all right.

I never want to experience the next ten minutes again. Ten minutes during which Michelle directed at me all the hurt, all the pain she must have been suffering, damning me for letting her down, for destroying, in one fell swoop, her good opinion of me, castigating me for forsaking my maternal role. Félix was right. A mistral had sprung up: the treacherous wind which appeared from nowhere to disrupt the heat of the summer day. *Le grand drawback de Provençe* had sneaked up on us while we were in the bedroom. Already it was whipping up the waves and blowing the sand along the terrace as Michelle told her mother what she thought of her, but the names that she called me were as nothing compared with the names I called myself.

There are some situations that cannot be retrieved, watches that cannot be put back. There was nothing I could say to redeem myself, nothing I could do to assuage the hurt Michelle was enduring. I stood by the sliding glass doors looking out at the flapping blinds, the grey-green sea, the bobbing sails as the wind, with its threat of violence, gusted in over the Garden of the Hesperides which so short a while ago had blossomed beneath a clear sky.

When Michelle had quietened I turned to talk to her, to try to explain that I had been possessed by forces beyond my control, to attempt to get her to understand the nature of my obsession, that I had not done, would never do, anything deliberately to harm her.

She was gathering up her rucksack, inserting her feet, with the fluorescent purple toenails that tugged on my heartstrings, clumsily into her flip-flops, drying her swollen eyes. I put out a hand to stay her but she looked right through me as if I did not exist, as if her gaze was fixed on the blue and white striped cushions which had been blown from the loungers and which were scudding along the terrace.

'Michelle . . . '

'Don't speak to me . . . ' Hiking her rucksack up on to her shoulders, she made for the door. 'Don't ever speak to me again.'

Knowing that it was useless, that there was nothing I could do, nothing I could say to alleviate the hurt, to mitigate the damage, I pulled my robe around me and let her go. For a brief moment I wished that I were dead.

I knew that it was not because she had been going out with Félix — Félix had told me they had never slept together — but because I had demolished her basic good opinion of me and deceived her father whom she loved and admired. It was a state of affairs which could not be rectified, a glass which had been shattered into a thousand pieces. I was aware of Félix standing beside me and was grateful that he did not touch me, did not try to tell me that everything was going to be all right.

The drive back to Paris was overshadowed by the turn that events had taken, a sombre finale to the joyful anticipation of the journey down. Félix had wanted to stay, to make the best we could of our last week, but I was frightened. I had to get back to Paris, to redeem what I could from the holocaust before, like the forest fires which, according to the latest reports, were sweeping through the Var and destroying everything in their paths, Michelle got back to Paris and the situation got irretrievably out of hand.

Félix did not really understand. Yes, it was embarrassing. Yes, he wished it hadn't happened, that Michelle had stayed away, but why deny ourselves what remained of our idyll? I put his obtuseness down to his youth and the fact that at twenty-eight the web that he weaved around himself was relatively untangled.

With the mistral still blowing, seeping under the doors and in through the window frames, leaving a yellow dust on the wicker chairs and the blue and white tiles, we stripped the bed of the sheets and our passion, closed the shutters, zapped the electricity and turned off the water supply. Shutting the door of Notre Rêve — which in the event had turned out to be a nightmare rather than a dream — behind us, we picked up our suitcases and made for the car.

They were the same sunflowers, the same avenues of limes when we left the autoroute, hissing their disapproval as we passed them by, the same perched villages on either side of us, little changed since the Middle Ages, the same motorway cafés with their melamine tables and ubiquitous *frites*, the same Routiers where we stopped for lunch among the HGV drivers and which I could not eat, but I saw none of it with the same eyes.

What if Michelle had already telephoned Jordan? Would I find my belongings already packed? Would Jordan, to whom the world, like that of his mother, was either black or white and whose morals were unassailable, throw me out? Had I, carried away by a *coup de foudre*, destroyed my family and everything I had invested in my marriage?

The diesel fumes which hung like a pall over Paris assaulted our noses and the night-time Péripherique, still gridlocked with traffic and dazzling with headlights, seemed to be never-ending.

On the corner of the Boulevard Courcelles, where I insisted Félix drop me, he followed me out of the car. The silent *manège* with its shrouded cars and miniature speedboats was bereft of children. We stood outside the illuminated window of the flower shop mocked by the grinning orange faces of the raffia pumpkins predicating Halloween. Félix took my hand.

'When will I see you?'

I wondered was he mad.

'I love you Judith.'

He loved my mature body, my maternal caring.

'It's over, Félix.'

'Not until the fat lady sings.'

Even now he could make me laugh. I picked up my suitcase.

'Call me. You will call me?'

His eyes were dark with passion. I yearned for him and knew that although a drastic operation, in the person of Michelle, had been carried out to relieve me of my sickness, I had not been cured.

I shook my head, glad that he could not see my tears. Had my suitcase not been so heavy I would have run, although I could not run away. Feeling like the criminal which I was — I had killed my marriage — I punched the keypad outside my building as the Merc disappeared into the distance.

Reluctant to face what might lie behind my own front door, I went first to Lauren's praying that she would be at home. Wearing a baby-doll nightdress and with the oily slick of night-cream on her surprised face she let me in.

'Do you know what the time is?'

'I need to talk.'

She stifled a yawn.

'If a girl needs to talk, a girl needs to talk.'

Leading the way into the mirrored sitting-room, she poured a glass of wine for each of us and, appraising my petrified face, curled up on one of the white sofas, awaiting my confession.

16

'When does Michelle get back?' Lauren said when I'd finished my story.

'The end of the week. What if she's already called Jordan?'

'Unlikely.'

'Possible.'

'Anything's possible,' Lauren shook her head. 'One indiscretion. *Bof!* Don't worry about it. Your husband is pure gold.'

'You've seen him?'

'You asked me to keep an eye on him. I invited him to dinner . . . '

'Dinner, you?' Lauren couldn't cook.

'I ordered a Chinese. Jordan brought his laptop, he worked most of the way through the Singapore noodles. Muttered about having to fix Monsieur le Viscomte . . . '

'He's run into problems with his deal.'

'I didn't ask for explanations. I've enough problems of my own. He did apologize. When he was through and I'd murdered an entire bottle of St Emilion, I said it had been a scintillating evening.'

'Jordan doesn't do sarcasm.'

'I told him he was the best looking man I

knew. I may have been a little drunk by that time.'

'And he said?'

'"Coming from you, Lauren, that's a compliment.' And I said, 'I wouldn't leave my husband in Paris on his own.' And he said, 'I didn't think you had a husband, Lauren.' And I said, 'Not for want of trying . . . "'

'Go on.'

'You really want me to? OK, I went to sit on the sofa beside him. And then I said — so help me God — 'if Judith wasn't my best friend, Jordan Flatland, I would take you into the bedroom and fuck you.'"

'And what did Jordan say?'

'Need you ask? He picked up his laptop, gave me a big hug, thanked me for the Singapore noodles, said he had an early start and kissed me goodnight. That's Jordan for you.'

'What am I going to do, Lauren?'

'For starters I suggest you kip down on that sofa. It's not a bit of use walking in on Jordan this time of night.'

'I mean what am I going to *do*?'

'Take one step at a time. Play it by ear.'

'What about the children. I don't want to lose the children.'

'Have you thought of the possibility that Michelle will keep this to herself and that it will all blow over?'

'How can I be sure?'

'You've got three days before she gets home. You'll work something out. It's two a.m., Judith. Some of us have to earn a living. Everything will look better in the morning.'

Lauren kissed me tenderly and lent me a toothbrush. To my surprise — I must have been exhausted by the rollercoaster of my emotions and from the journey — I slept.

★   ★   ★

When I let myself into my own apartment, Jordan was having breakfast as I knew he would be. He was a creature of precise habit and, by checking the time, I knew that he had already been for his jog. The *Allgemeine Zeitung* was on the kitchen table; he always stopped at the kiosk and picked up a newspaper for Helga.

I stood in the doorway of the time-expired kitchen as he poured milk on to his Granola. My heart was gyrating to an unfamiliar rhythm and I was uncertain of my reception.

'Judith!'

Why didn't he say 'darling'? Was he trying to tell me something? I need not have worried. He took me in his arms and whirled me around affectionately. I felt like Judas.

'Am I pleased to see you . . . '

'You missed me then?' I was still feeling my way.

'It's not so much that. I'm up to here — ' he indicated his chin ' — with wiener schnitzel!'

He poured me coffee, strong, as I liked it, and listened, wanting to know every detail while I filled him in on Antibes. Separating the wheat of the vacation from the chaff of Félix, I did my best to pick out the highlights: the sea, the weather, the food, the sights. I could have been reciting the merits of the Côte d'Azur verbatim from a travel guide. Jordan seemed not to notice. He told me about his trip to Boston where he had visited his mother on Beacon Hill and Maurice, our Weimeraner, in the boarding kennels. It wasn't hard to see from which one of them he had received the most rapturous welcome.

Kissing me again, he collected up his gear and glancing at his trusty Rolex made for the front door which I held open for him. 'By the way,' he pressed the button on the headstrong elevator, 'Michelle came home early. She didn't want to go to Juan without Lois. She's in her room.'

I tried to read his face but he was already in the elevator, disappearing inch by slow inch down to the ground floor. Did Jordan know? Was he playing games with me? I went into the apartment and closed the door.

'How's everything?' I asked Helga when she emerged, bleary eyed from her bedroom. I was trying to sound her out.

'Hans-Dieter is fine . . . '

'I meant with Mr Flatland?'

'Very gut!' A smile enveloped her face. 'He likes my wiener schnitzel.'

'How about Michelle?'

'Very sleeping. She say not to waken her up.'

Not falling over myself to 'waken Michelle up', I went into the bedroom where only Jordan's side of the bed was disturbed — he slept as tidily as he did everything else — and my Calvin Klein teeshirt, stained with suntan oil, lay where Michelle had apparently hurled it, contemptuously on my pristine pillow. I took a shower as leisurely as the erratic plumbing would allow and washed the salt water out of my hair. More than anything else I wanted to call Félix but it was, of course, out of the question. Feeling like an intruder in my own home, I set about clearing up the chaos that had accrued in the two weeks I had been away. I looked at the plate of anaemic veal escalopes in the otherwise empty fridge, cleaned the grease from where it had accumulated on the wall behind the cooker, and sorted through my mail. There was a postcard from Joey with a picture of a handsome leaping salmon on the front: 'Walter caught this ginormous salmon. He's going to have it smoaked.' There was a postscript from my mother to say that it was still raining but that everything was fine. I did not touch Michelle's rucksack which lay abandoned in the hall.

The day, which was languid and torrid — no mistral in Paris — passed languidly and torridly. Not knowing what to do with myself I listened outside Michelle's door for signs that she was stirring and waited with trepidation for Jordan to come home.

In the middle of the afternoon, after Helga had left for her English class, a wave of panic overtook me and I wondered whether Michelle was really asleep or if, tipped overboard by her discovery in Antibes, she had overdosed on something nasty. Opening her door quietly I looked into the bedroom where she was lying with her thumb in her mouth and breathing steadily. At five o'clock, because there was no food in the house and there was no way I was going to feed Jordan wiener schnitzel again, I went to the supermarket where my guilty conscience led me to spend a small fortune on baby artichokes and melons from Cavaillon and the finest quality *filet*. When I came out with my loaded trolley I looked in vain for the rose on my car.

Over dinner, which went unremarked on, Jordan brought me up to date with Rochelle Eléctronique. The session in Boston had been fruitful and he and Sherman had come back to Paris with a plan which was designed to appease the French Foreign Office so that the deal, with only minor amendments, could go ahead. They had presented their proposals to Monsieur le Viscomte and were waiting, not very patiently, for his response.

'I told him in no uncertain terms,' Jordan said over the steak which I had cooked almost to oblivion just as he liked it — Félix preferred his bloody and raw, 'that if they advised Rochelle against what we considered was an extremely fair proposal, more of a compromise than we would have liked, I have an alternative strategy which the French Government may find a good deal less congenial.'

'What alternative strategy?'

Jordan smiled; he was an ace bluffer.

'I haven't thought of one yet.'

I had bought some wine dark cherries, plump and fat, and we were eating them when Michelle appeared, dishevelled in not very clean shorts. Sitting down at the table and pushing aside her melon, she ignored my presence and turned to Jordan.

'Daddy, I need to talk to you.'

Thinking that the game was up and that she was going to tell Jordan about Félix, I got up to cook her steak and found that I was shaking.

Jordan took a brace of cherries joined by their stems from his plate and hung them over Michelle's ear as he had done when she was a child. She was not amused. Removing the earring and returning the cherries to his plate she said:

'I'm not coming back to Boston.'

'Is that so?' Jordan played for time. He liked to see all the cards on the table.

'I want to stay in Paris.'

'I had the impression you were going to law school in the fall.'

'I've changed my mind.'

Taking his memo-machine from his pocket Jordan rewound it and switched it to play.

'I suggest you discuss this with your mother,' he said, over the low volume of the recording from which I was able to distinguish the words Cavendish Holdings and Pilcher Bain.

'I suggest *you* discuss this with my mother.' Michelle's voice was caustic.

'Your father's very worried at the moment,'

I ventured, 'about Rochelle Eléctronique . . . '

Ignoring me disdainfully, which was no more than I deserved, Michelle addressed Jordan's back before storming out of the room.

'Maybe you should take your nose out of Rochelle Eléctronique some time!'

'What's gotten into her?' Jordan said later, when we were getting ready for bed.

When I didn't reply — I didn't trust myself — he went on:

'I wonder if it's something to do with that fellow.'

'What fellow?' I knew perfectly well.

'Félix? Didn't you say his name was Félix? He looked like a troublemaker. I didn't care for the look of him at the time.'

Since Jordan never liked the look of Michelle's boyfriends on principal, I did not defend him. I did not want to discuss Félix whose presence was never far from my mind.

'I saw Lauren while you were away,' Jordan said when we were in bed.

Honest John wanted to be sure that I knew he had done nothing underhand.

'She tried to get me into bed.'

Putting off the moment when I knew Jordan would want to make love to me, I joined in the conversation.

'She's been trying to get you into bed for years.'

'Well she didn't exactly try. She said if you weren't her best friend . . . '

You could always get an accurate picture from Jordan.

'I felt quite sorry for her. Look, I've missed you. I don't want to talk about Lauren.'

'Joey will be back in a few days.'

'And I don't want to talk about Joey. Did you miss me?'

I tried to take myself back to the Roman ruins of Provençe, to the elegant hotels and Palladian villas of *la Belle Époque*, to the fierce heat and the harsh light of the land of love immortalized by the troubadours and by the poetry of Petrarch, in which I had sojourned with my lover. No matter how poignant, how intense our experiences, like the pain of childbirth, they can never be accurately recalled.

Analysing it later I supposed that although I was no longer 'in love' with Jordan and his body could no longer claim to be a source of erotic delight, what I had with him was happiness and, until I met Félix, had wallowed in the security of living side by side with someone I felt I had known all my life. When I was with Jordan there was a sense of homecoming and the uncanny conviction that what there was between us was not a new experience but that we had met somewhere before. I loved Jordan and was in little doubt that I was wholeheartedly loved in return.

Why then, when he attempted to make love to me on my return from Antibes, did I turn away before thinking better of it and, not wishing to be unkind, submitted with my eyes closed — with Félix they were always open — to his caresses. When he touched me I floated unencumbered on the translucent sea; when he held my body, I looked up at the umbrella pines; when he entered me I was in a deserted cove, oblivious to the inroads into every orifice made by the coarse white sand.

'Good to have you back.' Sighing with satisfaction, Jordan kissed my forehead tenderly.

He was not to know that I could never, would never, return.

17

Looking back on it — my meeting with Félix at Michelle's birthday party, our time together in a separate world which only we inhabited — I attempted to convince myself that I had been in the grip of a mid-life crisis, and that Dr Katz had been right. Although I started at the sound of every motor-bike, jumped when the telephone rang and looked expectantly in unlikely places for the sight of a red rose, I tried to put the episode, my affair with Félix, behind me in the interests of my family, which could disintegrate at any moment, and my marriage. I did not realize how ill I was, and in the days that followed with no sign from Félix, all reason collapsed and my symptoms became progressively worse until my entire being was at their mercy. Although I talked to myself severely, telling myself what an idiot I was making of myself, my malady, which entailed suffering and pain unlike anything I had previously experienced, would not go away and I was at a loss to understand what it was doing to me and why. The nights were the worst and I tossed and turned, as if in the grip of a fever,

imagining my lover in bizarre and phantas-
magoric scenarios in which I did not figure,
or living it up with a panoply of nubile Kikis,
Natashas, Juliettes and Olympes.

I did call him from a call-box, my heart
pounding, but all I got was an answering
machine, on which there seemed to be a great
many messages judging by the beeps, and the
information that Félix Dumoulin was not
available *à ce moment* but would ring the
caller back. What with Michelle not talking to
me, and Jordan on a knife-edge waiting for an
answer from the Viscomte, the atmosphere in
the Boulevard Courcelles was tense.

Stupidly, regretting bitterly what had come
between us and optimistically hoping to
improve the situation, I had tried to square
things with Michelle. I explained to her,
woman to woman, that what appeared to be
unforgivable behaviour was due to circumstances entirely beyond my control, that it
was not my intention to hurt either her or her
father, but that the human heart was as
susceptible at forty-two as it was at eighteen,
and that the psyche did not age.

'I don't expect you to understand,' I said.

'You're dead right. I don't. I think you're
disgusting and I never want to have anything
to do with you again.'

Of course Jordan noticed what was going

on between us. When Michelle pointedly ignored me, or when I made the mistake of asking her to do something and she told me, impertinently, to do it myself, he took her to task for her rudeness and enquired what had gotten into her and what it was all about. She told him to 'ask Judith' — 'Mommie' or 'Mom' hadn't crossed her lips since we had been home — and sometimes she even referred to me, when she was addressing Jordan, as 'your wife'. Since she had outgrown teenage rebellion Jordan put her defiant attitude towards me, coupled with her insistence that she was abandoning her law degree and not coming back to Boston with us, down to the vicissitudes of her love-life. Little did he know that it was mine that was to blame.

On the morning that I was to fetch Joey from the airport — my mother and Walter were catching a plane straight back to the States — I noticed the Kawasaki with Félix sitting patiently astride it, waiting at the end of the street as I unlocked my car. We walked slowly towards one another and stood under a plane tree not daring to touch although there were few people about. He told me that there had been an urgent message waiting for him when he got home from Antibes, that he had been in Mulhouse, that his grandmother had had an operation.

'I did not dare to telephone. *J'ai beaucoup souffert.* When will you come?'

I did not answer immediately. I had intended to devote the next few days to Joey, to take him swimming and to the Jardin d'Acclimatation where there were ropes and a shooting-range. I had alienated my daughter and had no intention of alienating my son. The part of me that defined Judith Flatland as a rational human being realized that, standing under the plane tree with Félix, I had reached the point of no return, that I had had my summer and should have put an end to our folly there and then. Turning towards him, for I had been looking nervously up and down the street, I saw that he too was still in the grip of the malady with which I was consumed and in the face of which I was helpless. I was not responsible for the words that tripped feverishly off my demented tongue.

'I'll come tomorrow.'

★   ★   ★

Joey's delight in seeing me, and the fact that he had missed me, made up in part for Michelle's behaviour. He loved being with Grandma Pam and Walter, and had thoroughly enjoyed the fishing, but it was obvious from the way he regressed at bath-time, allowing me to wash his grimy neck which looked as if it hadn't been near a face-cloth since he had been away, that he was happy to be home. Picking up the threads of his life, he had already inveigled Jordan into allowing him to call his best friend, Ricky Judd, in Boston. He informed me, apropos of nothing, as I towelled him dry hugging him to me, that Ricky's parents were getting divorced.

'Ricky's going to live with his father,' Joey said.

'Why his father?' I rubbed his wet hair.

'His mother can't play baseball.'

To celebrate Joey's homecoming, Jordan put away his laptop and played regular Monopoly with his son. It was not just a game. It was about how to win in a modern world when your hotels are mortgaged and you can't pass Go. It educated you about life, taught you how to control your emotions and how, even if you were down to your last dollar and everyone else was winning, you don't give up. Jordan took every throw of the dice seriously, as he did everything, informing Joey as he amassed property after property, placing the Title Deeds face up in front of him before ending up in jail, that the three most important things to remember, as far as real estate was concerned, were location,

location, location, and that you needed luck to buy your properties but skill to manage them. He explained the minutiae of buying at auction, the best way to sell unimproved buildings, railroads and utilities in private transactions, the finer points of bankruptcy procedures and what action to take if the Bank, which could never go broke, ran out of money. Watching the two of them, one a carbon copy of the other, the same *louche* posture, the same blond quiff — although Jordan swore his hair was already receding — I tried to integrate them into the landscape of my mind, to make them part of me, but there was room for no one but Félix.

In the morning I asked Helga to take Joey to the Jardin d'Acclimatation. He did not seem to mind. I gave them money for pizzas and instructions that Helga was to keep her eyes on Joey at all times. When they had left the apartment, I watched them go down the street from the window; Joey seemed happy enough, taking six steps to Helga's one. I showered and put on my La Perla underwear and went to meet my lover.

What I liked about Félix and what I had missed while he had been away, was that even when we were thrown hither and thither on a sea of emotional turbulence, he didn't cut the thread of courtship, of gallantry, even of romance that lent vitality to our love. As I approached his studio I saw him looking anxiously out of the window for me as he fed the pigeons crumbs of stale *puits d'amour*: inside there was a red rose on every stair. I gathered them up, one by one, as I ascended, and the petals were crushed as he took me in his arms.

* * *

I had not intended to stay all day in the rue Dauphine but we were thirsty for each other, hungry for love. Later, entertained by street jugglers, we sat on wicker chairs outside the brasserie in the rue de Buci over an extremely late lunch which neither of us could eat. I was reluctant to go home.

When I put my key in the front door I expected to be assailed by an excited Joey eager to tell me of his adventure in the Jardin d'Acclimatation, but in the apartment only the gloom hit me. I called, then opened the doors. There was no Helga, no Michelle; their rooms were empty and although it was after six o'clock Joey was nowhere to be seen. I wondered what could have happened to them and was about to telephone Jordan at the office when the thought occurred to me that Helga had given into Joey's importuning and they had gone to see a film. I reckoned that they should be back within the hour, and turning on the radio to a jazz station on which they were playing *A Night in Tunisia*, set about preparing dinner.

I was assembling the salad which was to accompany the ham I had bought in the rue de Buci when I heard the front door open and rushed into the hall ready to castigate Helga for taking Joey to the cinema without my permission, without letting me know where they were. I was stopped in my tracks by the spectacle which confronted me.

Jordan, grim-faced, was putting his door keys on to the brass tray on the table, Helga, her hair awry, had been crying, and Joey, his arm in a sling, his teeshirt filthy and his cheek grazed, was white-faced and dishevelled.

Jordan was the first to speak.

'Where were you . . . ?'

'What's happened?' Running to put my arms around Joey, I didn't answer the question.

'I tried to call you.'

'I went to the dentist . . . ' the words came tumbling from my guilty tongue. 'I told you, I'm having this root canal treatment.'

I caught Jordan looking at me strangely, as I fiddled with Joey's sling to cover my confusion.

'Just a sprain,' Jordan's voice sounded terrible. 'Luckily it isn't broken.'

Piecing together the story I discovered that when Helga had taken Joey to the Jardin d'Acclimatation, he had shinned up one of the climbing ropes. Waving to Helga to demonstrate his prowess — typical Joey — his attention had wavered and his hand had slipped. He had fallen into the sandpit but had managed to knock his head on the side of the path. Because his mouth seemed to be bleeding profusely, a panic-stricken Helga had called for help and an ambulance had arrived to take him to hospital. Jordan had been summoned from the office in the midst of delicate negotiations with Claude Lafarge and he had had to spend the afternoon at the hospital where Joey's arm had been X-rayed before being strapped up. At the end of the day, when Joey was finally discharged, Jordan had taken him to the dental surgery where his broken tooth and bleeding mouth had been attended to. The dentist in question was Bob Latham, an American ex-pat whose practice was in the rue de Renard and to whom I had gone for a check-up when we first arrived in Paris.

Bathing Joey, taking care not to disturb his grazes, I asked him, my heart in my mouth, if 'Uncle Bob' as he called the dentist, had said anything about me.

'No.' Joey was squeezing water from the sponge on to his sore knee.

'Didn't he mention me?' I had to be sure.

'Daddy said, 'I hear Judith's been having trouble with her teeth lately' ' — the voice was Jordan's, Joey was a born mimic. 'You won't be cross with Helga will you, Mom? It wasn't her fault.'

'And what did Uncle Bob say?'

''I guess he'll live. If he takes care what he eats for a few days he'll keep the tooth too.''

'About me?'

The water ran in rivulets from the sponge.

''Tell her to make an appointment.''

Busy with Joey, with dinner which he couldn't eat, with pacifying Helga who refused to be pacified as if it was her fault that Joey had fallen, I managed to avoid a confrontation with Jordan who was on the phone to Sherman for most of the evening, until Joey was asleep and we faced each other in the salon.

Almost as shocked as Joey, Jordan told me grimly that after lengthy consultation, the Viscomte de Loisy had regretfully rejected the new proposal with which the Boston team had come up and that the situation, as far as Rochelle Eléctronique was concerned, remained unchanged.

'We gave the Viscomte one last chance to withdraw his insistence on the golden share.' Jordan's face was grim.

'And what did he say?'

'He said, 'I think the Foreign Office has made its position quite clear, Mr Flatland.' Fucking bastards!'

Jordan rarely swore, rarely lost his cool. My heart went out to him as he saw everything he had been working so hard towards for the past six months in danger of disintegrating. 'He's not going to get away with this.' He snapped open his laptop.

'You can hardly take on the French Foreign Office.'

'I'll take on the entire government if I have to.'

His face was tense with anger.

'I've got work to do, Judith. You go to bed.'

18

I was having lunch with Lauren. The *salon de thé* in its inauspicious courtyard had just reopened after the summer break and was packed with chattering women.

'I wish *I* was going back to Boston,' Lauren said over her Japanese tea in its distinctive silver pot. *'J'en ai ras le bol de Paris . . .'*

'What's wrong with Paris?'

'The place is old fashioned, the people are fifty years behind the times, the bureacracy is *insupportable* and the Bureau de Poste is beyond belief . . .'

Lauren had got it wrong. So much talent had been tapped, so many hearts had been fulfilled, so many powerful personalities had flowered in this city. Without Paris, Picasso would not be Picasso; without Paris, Chopin would not be Chopin; without Paris, Freud would not be Freud. Paris had made demands on them and they had lived up to her expectations.

'I'm not going back to Boston.'

'Excuse me? I presume you mean Michelle is not going back to Boston.'

'Jordan has persuaded Michelle to change

her mind. He told her she's going to be on that plane if he has to carry her on. Michelle is scared of Jordan. She knows that he means it. I'm the one not going back to Beacon Hill.'

'I suppose your toy boy's at the bottom of all this.'

'His name is Félix.'

'That's what he is, Judith. Your *cinq á sept*, your *liaison dangereux*, call it whatever you like. But not going back to Boston . . . Come on now, Judith!'

I had thought that Lauren, a woman of the world, would understand, but although she was a veteran of the dating trenches, I doubted if she had ever known love.

My decision had been made on the day after Joey's accident, when contrary to Jordan's instructions that I was to watch him like a hawk for the rest of the day in case he showed signs of concussion, I had sworn Helga to vigilance — nothing could go wrong in the apartment and I should not be gone long — and rushed into my lover's arms. I could not help myself. I could not. I knew that I should have stayed home with Joey who was perfectly happy playing with his Game Boy and watching his videos and enjoying the attention he was getting, but I had to get my fix of the mind-altering drug that was Félix.

In the rue de Buci I stopped at Carton to

buy mille feuilles, Félix's favourite, heavy with caramel and thick with pears. They were getting to know me in the quartier and, recognizing the familiar figures — the torch singer with her sequins, the old woman with her bag of clanking bottles, the transvestite with his long eyelashes, wobbling on his stiletto heels — I had begun to feel at home in the midst of the largely inviolate local life.

Félix was at his easel. He was painting, apparently from memory and in his own inimitable style, the *Lady with a Glove*: the oval of the face was still blank. He kissed my hand gravely, turning my legs to water.

We guzzled the mille feuilles I had brought as I fed him, at the easel, with the pastries. I told him about Joey, and about the accident, and my fabrication about my whereabouts which had been given the lie by the dentist.

'What did Jordan say?'

He had been too wrapped up in Rochelle Eléctronique. I hoped my falsehood had passed him by.

When we'd finished the mille feuilles, Félix threw down his brushes. We made love on the day-bed with its colourful Indian throw, then, frightened to stay in the studio any longer lest we forget the time again — I had told Helga I would not be gone long — and needing to get out of the stifling air, we walked down the rue

Dauphine until we reached the Seine where we strolled, among the other lovers, from the Pont Neuf to the Pont St Michel in the footsteps of André Breton, of Baudelaire, of Rilke, of Walter Sickert and of Wagner. Stone and water neither come into nor go out of fashion; the quays along which we passed were timeless and nothing had happened to change them.

'I'm not going to let you go back to Boston, Judith. Now that I've found you there is no way I can let you go . . .'

Standing on the quayside, watched by the tourists on the *bateaux mouches* when I should have been caring for my son, I considered his remark which I had long anticipated, and to which I had already acquiesced in my head. I tried to analyse what it was that drew me inexorably to Félix, like Juliet to Romeo, or Héloïse to Abelard, like so many star-struck lovers through the ages. It was like trying to analyse a painting, breaking its components down into so many square inches of canvas, so many brush strokes, so many tubes of paint. Like any beloved construct, Félix was greater than the sum of his physical presence, of his caring and romantic parts.

'You will have to tell Jordan . . .'

He made it sound easy to surrender my life on a plate.

'Will you tell him?'

It was impossible to talk to Jordan at the moment. He was interested in nothing other than rescuing his deal.

'He will have to be told sooner or later.'

Sooner or later Jordan would have to be told.

On the way back to the rue Mazarine where I had parked my car, we passed a boutique with a notice in the window: '*recrute vendeuse*', beside a flounced, flame-red dress on a supercilious model with a chalk-white face. Félix had his arm around my shoulders. Drawn by the dramatic impact of the presentation, we stopped to stare.

'I'd like to buy it for you.'

Jordan had never so much as entered a dress shop.

I told him that according to Lauren, black was the new black.

'Then you will stand out like a cardinal among a flock of priests.'

In the shop, whose bell tinkled as we entered summoning the *vendeuse* who wore a diamond ring on her engagement finger, I tried on the scarlet dress while Félix sat patiently on a chair.

'It's not my colour.'

I felt like the Scarlet Woman, like Scarlet O'Hara, the Woman in Red.

It fitted me perfectly: voluptuous, bare backed, the flounces undulating as I moved. Women who wore red were perceived to be bad news. Holding my head high I confronted the new Judith Flatland who regarded me from the mirror.

Straightening a seam here, a flounce there, the *vendeuse* signified her approval. As if we were alone in the shop, Félix kissed my exposed flesh, his mouth lingering on my back, and indicated that we would take it.

'*Que tu es belle, Judith. Que tu es belle.*'

★   ★   ★

'Let me tell you something, Judith,' Lauren's face was serious. 'I speak to you as a friend.'

Wondering what was coming I put my fork down on my smoked-salmon blinis.

'You have to eat,' Lauren said. 'You're making yourself ill.'

I was ill, sick with love. I kept my mouth shut.

'How old are you Judith?'

'You know perfectly well how old I am. I'm forty-two. I'm the same age as you.'

'And how old is your . . . ' she caught my eye, 'Félix.'

'Félix is twenty-eight. Our birthdays are in February. We are both Aquarians.'

Lauren snorted.

'Big deal. Have you thought what things are going to be like in twenty years time when you are sixty-eight; when you are old and Félix is in his prime?'

'What's that got to do with anything?' I refused to think about it. I had fallen in love with Félix and it was the best thing and the worst thing I had ever done.

'Have you thought about Jordan?'

'Jordan's married to the bank.'

'Jordan would never take you back.'

Lauren was probably right. Like a broken friendship, a betrayed trust, my relationship with Jordan, once severed, could never be reinstated.

'Have you thought about your children?'

'Michelle no longer needs me. She no longer talks to me.'

'Joey is *nine* years old.'

'Joey is a survivor.'

It was true. He was dependent on nobody and was already planning the trip he was going to take round the world when he left school.

'How will he manage without you?'

'It's only Paris, Lauren. I'm still his mother.'

'You're in a bubble, Judith. Someday that bubble is going to burst . . . '

I would have to take that chance. Although somewhere I knew that Lauren was talking sense, that she had my interests at heart, I could not endow her words with any sort of meaning.

'Take anyone out of their usual environment and madness will ensue. What is it with this young man, Judith?' Lauren was getting desperate. 'Don't give me that crap about sex. Sex doesn't last — take it from Momma — we'd all die from exhaustion if it lasted forever.'

'It's how he makes me feel.'

It was true. When I was with Félix I no longer felt chronically undervalued. I was worthy of consideration, someone in her own right.

'You got married too young.'

I remembered my wedding day. I had married Jordan not only because I loved him but because he made me feel safe. He was the one for me and I had let him persuade me that I was the one for him. Neither of us saw any reason why we shouldn't make it official straight away. Looking round the congregation in the church and seeing my friends grinning at me in their new hats and hired morning coats, I did wonder how it was that I had reached this pivotal moment in my life so soon.

'What are you trying to say?'

'I'm not trying to say anything, Judith. You have tunnel vision. I might as well save my breath.'

It was Nadine, little Nadine with her chic little clothes and her gamine hair — on Beacon Hill it was said that if Nadine fell down a drain she would come up smelling of violets — when she came to discuss the menu for the farewell dinner, who told me about Rochelle Eléctronique, who put me in the picture about Jordan's Machiavellian scheme.

Kicking off her size three shoes and making herself as comfortable as she could on the unyielding Genoese cut-velvet sofa in the salon with its walls hung with yellow silk and its lacklustre eighteenth-century paintings of Frenchmen of good family leaving home to join the army, she said:

'You're not going to believe this, Judith, but your husband is holding the French Government to ransom!'

'Nothing that Jordan does would surprise me.'

'Wait till you hear this. Jordan has given the Viscomte one week to back down. To reconsider his proposal concerning the golden share. If Jordan doesn't hear directly from the Foreign Office before noon next Wednesday, that they are prepared to go ahead with Rochelle Eléctronique *on the basis originally agreed*, he's going to take the matter into his own hands.'

'What did the Viscomte say to that?'

' ''That is entirely up to you Mr Flatland.'' '

At this point the Viscomte had apparently got up from his chair and indicated that the meeting was at an end. Jordan had insisted that he not only sit down again and listen, but listen extremely carefully to what he was about to say.

If Nadine had got the story right — and there was no reason to suppose that she had not — if there was no word from the Foreign Office by the time Jordan's deadline had expired, he intended to put the plan he had devised into motion, to hit them where it hurt. On Wednesday morning, sealed envelopes containing invitations to a press conference at Offenbach Frères at 6 p.m., would be delivered by courier to the principal financial journalists in Paris. The Viscomte had refused to be intimidated. 'Ze Foreign Office has nossing to fear from ze press.'

'Wait till you hear this, Judith. Jordan will mark the envelopes, 'Not to be opened until 3.30 p.m.' — *after* the stock exchange has closed. At the press conference, Jordan will tell the reporters how Pilcher Bain has been treated in Paris and will make it clear to them that as a direct consequence of the French Government's outrageous and unacceptable last minute demands, his client will be pulling out of the Rochelle Eléctronique deal!'

I could not believe that Jordan, who had worked so hard for so long, was prepared to walk away from the deal.

'What was the response?'

'Zilch. It was the next bit that wiped the smile off the Viscomte's face.'

While the invitations were being delivered, Nadine said, some of them could 'accidentally' be dropped and fall into the wrong hands *while the Bourse was still open.*

I was getting confused.

'So?'

'Rochelle Eléctronique is a blue-chip company. If it gets out that Pilcher Bain has called a press conference because the French Government is blocking a bid, the value of the shares would drop sharply. The Bourse could get jittery about the government's behaviour and institutional investors might well decide to switch their funds out of French markets. The last thing Monsieur le Viscomte wants to do is to jeopardize the position of Paris in the financial league table. Sherman thinks Jordan has gone bananas.

'The Viscomte is beside himself. He's accused Jordan of blackmail, told him that the government is not prepared to be put under pressure and, in addition, has threatened to make a formal complaint, not only to Pilcher Bain in Boston, but to the United States treasury department . . . '

'Good God!'

'That's not all. He's going to make a strong recommendation to his government that Jordan, Sherman, and the bank be barred from ever doing business in France again. I knew Jordan was tough, Judith, but even Sherman is worried and he knows him pretty well. Who was it said that we die without really knowing what the person closest to us is capable of?'

When Nadine had finished her story I realized why Jordan, who usually kept me informed of what was going on at the bank, had this time not confided in me. At least I presumed that was the reason. All he had told me was that he was putting the screws on the Viscomte and that if Claude Lafarge called and wanted to speak to him — no matter how urgently — at any time of the day or night before next Wednesday, he was out.

'About the menu,' Nadine said.

'The menu?'

'For the celebration dinner. I've found the most divine caterer . . . '

'Is there going to be a celebration dinner?'

Knowing Jordan, knowing his capacity for taking risks, for taking everything to the very edge, his absolute integrity, his abhorrence of being double-crossed or of double-crossing, I thought that there was every chance there might be.

19

In the end we settled on an iced soup in consideration of the weather, followed by *gigot d'agneau*, and a Grand Marnier soufflé for which the caterer Nadine had found was famed.

While Nadine, wearing her *Anyoccasion-.com* hat and writing everything down in a spiral notebook, waxed lyrical about the dinner — did I think canapés to start and what about the champagne? — I was wondering how I was going to tell Jordan of my decision, and if the Rochelle Eléctronique deal were to fall through, would I be strong enough to deliver the *coup de grâce*, and my thoughts were elsewhere.

It is one thing deciding to leave your husband and quite another thing to do it. Since I had made my mind up I had made several abortive attempts to discuss the matter with Jordan whom I knew would not only be disbelieving, but would be profoundly shocked. How did you tell someone who loved you, who was the father of your children, with whom you were intimate and had shared everything for eighteen years, that it was all over? Had there been a book I would have taken it out of the library; had there been a manual on how to leave your husband after eighteen years of marriage in which the treacherous bends and stretches of white water had largely been weathered, I would have consulted it. I begged Lauren to advise me but since she thoroughly disapproved of the action I was contemplating she refused to help.

'It's not as if you don't love Jordan, Judith.'

'There are many kinds of love.'

'What you and Jordan have going for you is the ongoing kind. From where I'm standing it's been a pretty sensational journey.'

'People who set out together are not necessarily the same after ten years, let alone eighteen.'

'I wish I could make you see sense.'

I knew that it was commonplace to love one person and be 'in love' with another, and that once the heart is set, the lover will listen to no warnings, no advice.

'Perhaps eighteen years is too long to be sensible. There's no fun in being sensible. Perhaps I'm bored.'

'Bored is no reason to ditch a marriage.'

'How would you know?'

'You don't have to be a chef to judge an omelette.'

Lauren always had an answer.

'Bored is nothing. Lonely is something. Ask all the lonely people. Lonely is the worst scenario.'

'I'm not going to be lonely.'

'Without Michelle? Oh I know she's not talking to you at the moment, she'll get over it. Without Joey? Without your dried up stick of a mother-in-law, without your job in the museum and your colleagues, without the gym, without the tennis club, without Jordan, even if he has he got takeovers for eyes, without your life on Beacon Hill?'

I let Lauren talk. It was like a chimera. All I could see was Félix and Beacon Hill seemed far away.

Plucking up my courage — it was not an easy thing to do — I tried, on more than one occasion, to broach the subject with Jordan. I thought it only fair. Each time we were interrupted and I finally gave up, putting off the evil I was about to do until the day thereof.

On the first two occasions, as if it were part of a conspiracy to silence me, we were interrupted by the telephone which I had instructions to answer in case it was Claude Lafarge.

I waited until Jordan seemed a little less tense than he had been of late as he waited for word from the Viscomte. Guessing what he must be going through, with his career, with everything he had worked so hard for on the line, I made him sit down in the salon after Joey had gone to bed.

'I need to call a meeting . . . '

It was a joke between us. I'd schedule a meeting so that I could be sure of his full attention whenever I had some domestic matter — fixing to have the house redecorated or Joey's school report or Michelle's unacceptable behaviour — to discuss.

'I need to talk to you.' I ignored my heart which was thumping away.

'OK, what's on the agenda?' His amused smile belying the anxiety in his eyes, his permanently drawn face, he joined in the game.

I got as far as taking a deep breath and saying:

'There's something we have to talk about. Something extremely important. You're not going to — '

I was about to say, 'You're not going to like it', when the telephone rang.

It was Charles Whittaker from the treasury department in Boston. Jordan grabbed the receiver. I heard him say, 'Yes sir . . . Yes sir, he said he would . . . No sir . . . No sir, it's the oldest trick in the book and I have no intention of letting them pull it . . . I'm glad I have your support and will proceed as planned . . . Yes sir . . . of course I will, sir . . . Accidents however do happen . . . Let's hope they won't be necessary.'

The call lifted his mood, he looked happier than he had done for days. Before I knew it he was on his mobile to Sherman, reporting his conversation with the treasury department, tearing it apart, and the moment was lost.

The second time I tried to bring up the subject of Félix, it was Claude Lafarge insisting that he speak to Jordan on a matter of extreme urgency. Aware of my instructions, I put my hand over the receiver.

'He says it's extremely urgent.'

Jordan shook his head.

'I'm sorry, Monsieur Lafarge, my husband is out.'

I put my hand over the receiver again.

'He wants to know when it will be convenient to talk to you.'

This time Jordan left the room and I relied on my own ingenuity to spin a tale about him having to leave Paris for a few days, having to go to Mulhouse, although of course that was Félix.

In the end it was Félix who helped me to nullify my marriage, to cut the ties that bound me inextricably to my life.

Time was rapidly running out and Jordan still had not heard from the Viscomte. The muscles in his cheek were twitching, and recognizing the danger signal I was careful not to cross him. He was sharp with Joey which was unusual, and the sound of the telephone, which put him on full alert, made him jump. It was not an easy time for either of us.

Hot as it was in the rue de Buci, the *quartier* which I knew by sight, by sound, by smell, and of which I already felt part, grew more beautiful. In the mysterious de Chirico shadows, pierced by tumbling urns of busy lizzies, and the vanishing points of the cul-de-sac, could be seen the architectural follies, the intricate intimacies of the buildings, the *clochards* slumped motionless in the doorways, the urine trickling from behind builders' skips — there were not enough *pissoirs* — which mingled with the animal scent left by cats and coiffured poodles and ran in rivulets into the road.

Félix needed some paints to finish his portrait. The *Lady with a Glove* was almost completed. The filligree of the dress which spanned her narrow waist was as black as the original in the Musée d'Orsay; like her prototype she seductively removed her

239

remaining glove, the little finger extended; this time, however, the titled face unmistakeably bore my features and the rose in her hat was red.

Although I had not sat for the portrait, I knew, from watching Félix, a painter obsessed by the fundamental eccentricities of his subjects, that the pigment had been vigorously handled, as if the canvas were a battle-ground, and that the strength of the likeness testified both to his feelings towards me and to the inner struggle which informed the completion of the work.

Sennelier, on the Quai Voltaire across the river from the Louvre, was an ancient mecca for artists' materials. In the windows were unsullied easels, boxes of acrylics, watercolour papers and *mannequins articulés* gesticulating to the passers-by with their stiff wooden limbs, while inside, in ordered chaos, were varnished wood cabinets, brass-handled drawers with illegible labels, coloured inks and pigments and plaster casts of classical heads illuminating the gloom. While Félix made his selection from the violets, ochres, magentas and ivory blacks of the *couleurs à l'huile* in pristine tubes, discussing his needs with the knowledgeable assistants in their white cotton coats, I fingered the brushes, 'Raphaels' and 'Manets' in all sizes and substances, from the finest sable to the coarsest bristle, touched the fans of creamy paper, the sketch pads and albums and the rolled *toiles écrues*. A case of hand-moulded pastels laid end to end in tempting sticks of ethereal colours — lemons and umbres for landscapes, pinks and browns for por-traits, rose and crimson for flowers — conjured up Boucher, Degas and Pascin, their delicate strokes as fragile as gossamer.

Carrying our purchases we crossed the road to where the *bouquinistes* were laying out their stalls with crude facsimiles of the Sacré Coeur and paperback translations of Henry Miller. Descending the steps of the Escale Malaquais and, as if we had all the time in the world, we melded with the other lovers walking arm-in-arm beneath the poplar trees, skirting the joggers and the silent pony-tailed fishermen in their battle fatigues standing guard over hopeful rods. The slopping water and the intricate patterns of the Louvre were picked out by the sunlight, and the mournful siren of a passing barge festooned with geraniums and washing-lines was drowned by the raucous commentary that came from the bows of a swiftly moving sightseeing boat.

I knew what whom one meets, and when, and where, lay largely in the juggling hands of chance, that our eye contact at Michelle's

241

birthday celebration had activated a network in my brain which made an instant decision as to the desirability of such contact, and that 'falling in love' was no way of getting to know someone. No one could take away from us, however, the tall blue days of the past few weeks, nothing could obliterate them. Despite the fact that, according to Lauren, our relationship glittered with illusion, provided no accurate map of reality, no authentic guide to the future, I was certain that, whatever defeats or failures we encountered, it was destined to succeed.

On the corner of the rue de Buci there is a plaque which reads:

ICI À ÉTÉ TUÉ
FRED PALACIO
CORPS FRANC VICTOIRE
CDLR.
POUR LA LIBÉRATION DE PARIS
LE 19 AOÛT 1944
A L'ÂGE DE 21 ANS.

It made me shiver. Félix put his arm around me. When we opened the heavy door and climbed up to the studio, the Boulevard Courcelles with its bourgeois face and its prissy wrought iron balconies retreated into the distance. It was as if I had come home.

Félix was arranging the metal tubes he had bought neatly into his wooden, paint-stained box.

'I can't do it,' I said.

'Can't do what?'

'I can't tell Jordan.'

'Send him a fax.'

'Honestly, Félix, I've tried.'

'What's the problem?'

'He's in big trouble with the Foreign Office.'

'You want *me* to tell him?'

'You'd do that, wouldn't you?'

'I'd swim the Hellespont ... Are you crying, Judith?'

'I'm not crying. I'm weeping.'

Félix looked bewildered.

'There is a difference?'

'Weeping is a private affair.'

Drying my eyes with his handkerchief, Félix led me to the sofa.

'Nothing is private between us.'

'I can't bear to hurt him.'

'Jordan will get over it. *Je te promets* ... '

He smoothed the hair back from my forehead, kissed my damp face until his lips were damp, pulled down the zipper of my summer dress.

'Even when I look like the back end of a bus you make me feel like Madonna ... '

'You'll tell him tomorrow.'

'Tomorrow is Wednesday. By midday he has to hear from Claude Lafarge.'

I knew that whether the Rochelle Eléctronique deal was on or off, time was running out. If the deal was on, Jordan would be busy signing contracts, then it would be straight into packing up the Boulevard Courcelles as Jordan was needed in Boston. If the deal collapsed, Jordan would be devastated and I doubted if I would have the strength to add fuel to the fire of his defeat.

I dismissed the alternatives from my head and concentrated on my lover, clinging desperately to my new life. I was not disappointed. With Félix I was never disappointed, as every act of love revealed new strata in the unworked seams of our passion.

Happy, in what seemed the perpetual sunlight that came through the open windows, in the separate world that we inhabited, we lay in each other's arms.

'Better?'

I kissed his forehead.

'Doctor Dumoulin, with a cure for everything.'

'I do my best.'

But he could not tell Jordan, could not surmount the obstacles that stood in the way of our love, highlighting its attractions, as if they did not exist. Would Romeo and Juliet, if not constrained by parental opposition, have been compelled to invent it? But if Félix was Romeo, Judith Flatland — while possessed of equal determination, equal consuming ardour and desire — was not, by any stretch of the imagination, Juliet. How could I explain to my lover that while the very essence of him had permeated my soul, being with him entailed wounding someone I loved and who loved me, hurting my children, throwing a lighted match on to the bonfire of my former life.

'It's simple enough, Judith.' Félix held me very close. 'The drawbridge is down.' Sometimes his youth betrayed him. 'All you have to do is walk.'

20

All you have to do is walk . . .

Félix was right, but it was like talking to a crawling infant, instructing it to stand up and put one foot in front of the other, as if it were that simple, as if there were not muscles to be strengthened, balance to be attended to, brain cells to be developed, the necessary maturity to be achieved.

There were women I knew who could have left the Boulevard Courcelles with their suitcases without turning a hair, without a backward glance. I was not one of them.

On Tuesday night, twelve hours before the Viscomte de Loisy's option ran out on the Rochelle Eléctronique deal, it should by rights have been Jordan who was unable to get any rest. While I lay wide awake in the heat in the *lit-bateau* covered only by a sheet — the temperature had not dropped all day — he slept, stripped to the waist, like the proverbial log.

In the morning, waiting for the Viscomte's call that would surely tell him the government had retracted and the deal could go ahead, he did not go for his customary jog. Strained in every nerve and sinew by the phantasmagoria of the night which had been filled with distorted and grotesque images, I hovered in the kitchen while Jordan had breakfast, unsure whether to make one more attempt to tell him. It was not the time, not the moment. I felt like an assassin with his knife.

When the telephone rang he almost spilled his coffee. It was Nadine with a query about the celebration dinner which, Jordan was convinced, would not have to be cancelled. I told her I would call her back.

'If you don't hear from the Viscomte by midday,' I could not meet Jordan's eyes, 'will there really be an 'accident'? Will you really let the invitations to the press conference fall into the wrong hands?'

I was making conversation with a man to whom I had been married long enough to read the answer in his eyes. I knew that he would stop at nothing in the face of perceived injustice. If necessary he would see the Bourse crash. He would bring the French Government down. I could not but admire his unfaltering courage and determination and wished that mine could match it.

I followed him about nervously as he made his determined preparations to leave for the bank where the invitations to the Pilcher Bain press conference, the top one addressed to the financial editor of *Le Monde*, lay on his desk, ready to be delivered.

For the last time I watched my husband of eighteen years, my lover, my companion, my friend, brush his blond hair before the bathroom mirror, take his coat from its hanger in the inadequate armoire, tie the statutory tie loosely round his neck, put a clean handkerchief in his pocket, collect his laptop and his organizer and his diary and his gold pen and pencil and his two mobile telephones and walk toward the door of our apartment, towards one of the most significant days of his forty-five-year-old life.

'Jordan . . . '

He looked at his gold Rolex.

'Not now, darling. If it's about the dinner tonight, I leave it entirely to you.'

At the door he turned and kissed me, more tenderly than usual.

'Love you. I'll always love you . . . '

I wondered if he knew.

'Call you from the office.'

Nadine wanted to go over the final arrangements for the dinner, which might, or might not go ahead as planned. I was in no mood to hear about iced soup and gigot and Grand Marnier soufflé for a celebration in which I would not be participating. I spent half the morning composing a letter to

Jordan. The second half I spent tearing it up. When the telephone rang at one minute to twelve, I ran into the hall.

'Judith?'

It was Félix.

'*Que je t'aime . . .* '

I cradled the receiver to my cheek.

'When will you come?'

'I have to wait for the caterer. I'll be there by six.'

At one o'clock I called the office. In the background I could hear excited laughter and the popping of champagne corks.

'The Viscomte has backed down!' Eunice sounded drunk with excitement although I knew she did not drink. I heard her in muffled conversation. 'Jordan will be home at six.'

What did one wear to walk out on one's marriage? I searched the cupboard for a dress to suit the occasion and hung it, black — for mourning — and virginal white, on the mahogany cheval-glass while I packed, smiling because I was going to Félix and I could not wait to feel his arms around me, and crying because it was so hard. The teeshirts and the skirts and the shorts and the jeans blurred before me and Jordan would not have approved of the way I flung them higgledy-piggledy into the case. I didn't really care. If they were not the clothes I needed I would buy others, tailoring them to my new life. Fortunately, I did not need to worry about money — Jordan had seen to that. There were bonds and shares in my name and I had enough to live on without being dependent upon Félix. Later, although I knew that Parisians did not care for Americans in general, I would get a job at the Musée d'Orsay or the Jeu de Paume where I guessed I would be in demand, walk home with my baguette, and make cheating cassoulet for dinner.

I had arranged with Helga to take Joey swimming; I told her it was to leave the way clear for the caterers who would be taking over the kitchen.

When it was time for them to go, Joey was still in his room with his face in a comic.

'Helga's waiting to take you to the pool.'

'OK.' He put down his comic.

'Are you looking forward to going home?' I sat down on the bed beside him.

'You know the first thing I'm gonna do when I get back to Boston?'

'You tell me.'

'I'm gonna have a chocolate chip ice-cream with hot butterscotch sauce. Helga's gonna have a Bananafanna Sundae. She can't even say Bananafanna Sundae!'

The innocence of small boys . . . I stroked his hair, blond like Jordan's.

'I want you to promise me something. I want you to promise me to practice the César Franck — '

His face fell. 'You said I could go swimming, Mom.'

' — when you get back to Boston.'

He didn't notice — Joey wouldn't — the tears in my eyes.

When they were ready to leave, I said:

'Look after Joey, Helga.'

She thought I meant at the *piscine*.

'Of course. We have a gut time, ja Joey!'

'Goodbye Joey . . . '

'Bye Mom.' He was halfway to the elevator with his Dalek backpack.

'I love you.'

I saw Joey roll his eyes up to the ceiling as he got into the elevator and pressed the button which carried him slowly away.

The catering team, surly but polite, comprised a fierce-looking chef in checked trousers with a fine *balcon* of a bosom, a young assistant with a ring through his nose clomping around in Doc Martens, and a diminutive oriental. At five o'clock they swept into the kitchen bearing plastic crates of goodies concealed beneath pristine white cloths. I showed them the buffet in the

251

dining-room with the baize-lined drawers of monogrammed silver, the musty-smelling cupboards of neatly ranged crystal — a glass for every wine — explained the idiosyncrasies of the cast-iron range, for which I got a condescending smile and a rapid salvo of '*Oui madames*' for my pains.

I was still worrying about leaving a note for Jordan, when I noticed that in his agitation about the Viscomte — and I read it as a pointer to his true state of mind beneath his deceptively calm exterior — he had left his memo-recorder by his bed.

Switching it on I heard his familiar voice:

' . . . Undertake never to force them into any deal that could be construed to threaten the security of France. Any disagreement to go to arbitration . . . '

I took a deep breath.

'Jordan, it's me, Judith. I'm not coming back to Boston. I've tried to talk to you about Félix but you wouldn't listen. Félix is the one you met at Michelle's birthday party, the one with the Kawasaki . . . '

The one who had taken the life of Judith Flatland and turned it on its head. The one with whom I am insanely, hopelessly, rapturously, shamelessly, agonizingly in love. The one without whom I am unable to contemplate life. The one without whom I cannot live.

'Strangely enough, Jordan, this has nothing whatever to do with you. I don't blame you. You have done nothing wrong. You have always been a good husband, a good father, and you have to believe I still love you, but not in the same way that I love Félix, to the very depths of my being, to the very limits of my soul. I won't go on about him because I know that by the time you get this far you will be angry, very angry. You've never been afraid of confrontation — you weren't afraid of the Viscomte — and you'll probably want to kill Félix. Or me. Or both of us. I don't know. But I implore you to forgive me. To forgive us. I wouldn't do the least thing to hurt you if I could help myself but at the risk of sounding maudlin I have to say that I cannot — believe me Jordan, I've tried and I cannot — help myself. You don't need me in the same way that Félix needs me. Michelle is disgusted with me; I think you'd better ask her why, I'm sure she'll tell you. And Joey . . . my darling Joey . . . Leaving Joey is the hardest part but Joey is a survivor.

'I am going to live in Paris. Much as I love Boston, I love the sights, the sounds, the smells, here. Paris is a city in which people matter and already I feel part of the place where Félix has his studio. Later we will divide our time between the *quartier* and the

Pas de Calais. There is no point in going on, Jordan, because you really won't be listening to the rationale of all this. There is no rationale. Perhaps acting on impulse, on intuition, knowing what you must do but not why you are doing it, is one of the secrets of happiness. You are right to be angry. It's a dreadful thing to do but there is no other way than to do it. One day perhaps you will understand and forgive me. I don't expect you to do that now. I can't talk any more. I have made the decision. Don't think it's easy. There is no rewind button. I do love you. But to think that you can love only one person for the whole of your life is like expecting a candle to burn forever. You get married when you're young, then you find out what it is you really want, what you've been looking for, what makes you happy, what you need. Please don't send the gendarmerie after me . . . Please . . . no, nothing. I'll be in touch.'

Putting the memo-recorder back by Jordan's bed, I wondered, irrationally if, now that I was gone, he would make the middle reaches of the *lit-bateau* his own.

At five-thirty I told the caterers that I was going to the hairdresser, and that Nadine would be along soon. Picking up my heavy suitcase, I put a farewell hand on Jordan's pillow, I glanced for a moment at the chaos

254

left on her floor by Michelle who was still not speaking to me, and stood for a long time, inhaling the distinctive smell of small boy, in Joey's bedroom. I was on my way to the front door when there was a crash of glass.

'*C'était un accident, madame*,' the little oriental girl was in tears as she brushed the shards from the Turkish rug. I thought the buxom chef was going to kill her and told the girl not to worry, there seemed enough crystal left in the cupboard to furnish a banquet. Leaving them screaming at each other among the mountains of unshelled peas and bunches of baby carrots and uniform marble-sized potatoes, I took a deep breath and walked out of the apartment and away from my life.

★   ★   ★

In the yellow Renault, driving on automatic pilot as I made my way across the river to the rue de Buci, I tried to come to terms with the draconian step I was taking. I would no longer go back to the Boulevard Courcelles; I would no longer go back to Boston; I would no longer be the nucleus surrounded by the atoms of my family; I would no longer be Jordan's wife. I tried to be miserable but could not summon up the necessary emotion and my heart was singing a spontaneous song

255

as I made my way to my young lover.

My daydream was interrupted by a second shattering of glass and I had the impression I was back in the apartment as I slammed on the brakes narrowly avoiding the car in front of me. I saw that there had been an accident ahead, causing a pile-up of traffic, and unbuckling the seat belt which had certainly prevented me from hitting my head on the windscreen, I got out of the car to see what had happened.

A few onlookers had already assembled and were staring silently at something in the road. Pushing my way to the front of the semi-circle, I followed their horrified eyes to the pool of blood in which a boy, the same age as Joey, lay twisted and motionless, still clutching a baguette. A young man kneeled beside him, expert fingers seeking a pulse, searching frantically for signs of life. Impervious to the blood staining his trousers, he removed the bread from the boy's hand and gently closed his eyes.

Picking up the Game Boy which no one had noticed and which had scudded into the gutter near me, and vaguely aware of the sound of an approaching ambulance siren, I leaned against a gnarled tree which rose from a weed-filled grating and threw up.

What seemed a long while later, a

bystander asked if she could help me and if I had been hurt. I reassured her that I was all right and enquired, stupidly, after the boy. They were shutting the doors of the ambulance and the crowd was dispersing silently. The woman looked at me sympathetically, and sympathetically shook her head.

21

In the rue de Buci, I sat in the café with Félix where, refusing to go up to the studio, I had insisted he meet me.

I waited while the familiar waiter set down two Pernods and the check which with the dexterity of a *prestidigitateur* he secured beneath the ashtray.

'It's over, Félix. I thought I loved you . . . '

'*Thought* you loved me?'

'It was an interlude. A summer interlude.'

I took a deep breath.

'I made a mistake.'

Félix looked bewildered. 'What are you talking about? I don't understand.'

'Us. You and me. It was an affair. A *cinq à sept*.'

'What happened?'

'Nothing happened.' I had been expelled from paradise. 'I made a middle-aged fool of myself.'

Withdrawing my fingers as Félix reached for them, I was glad that he could not see the invisible tears that choked me behind my shades. I picked up my glass which was damp with condensation, needing something to do with my hands.

'I thought we were happy.'

'Perhaps human beings don't need to be happy. Perhaps they aren't meant to be.'

'You're angry about something. Are you angry with me?'

I shook my head.

'This has to do with Jordan.'

I recalled the covenant I had made with Jordan and my heart which so short a while ago I had given to Félix.

'It has nothing to do with Jordan.'

'If you go back to Boston, Judith, my life is finished . . . '

I wondered would Félix kill himself like other spurned lovers. Would he turn his face to the wall and perish. Would he lose his mind and do something terrible. Would he walk out into the snow and die.

'I can't live without you, Judith.'

Witnessing his suffering I felt my own despair, the sensation of guilt which accompanied the withdrawal of my love, overwhelm me.

'Don't make it . . . difficult.'

'Difficult! You want me to make it easy? I love you. *Je t'aime, tu comprends?* The two of us together. Your body next to mine . . . You think love goes away because you ask it to?'

There was no answer to the question, or the answer was so atavistic, so deeply submerged that it was as good as buried.

I finished my Pernod.

'*Il faut que je m'en aille.*'

'You can't go. I love you . . . '

I looked at my watch.

'Jordan wants dinner early?' There was fury in Félix's voice.

'It's a celebration dinner. Jordan has pulled off his deal.'

I touched Félix's arm beneath the rolled-up sleeves of his shirt. It nearly did for me. Drops of water fell on to the dimpled aluminium table. I looked up at the gathering clouds thinking that it must be raining.

'You love me, Judith.'

Summoning up my strength I pushed back my wicker chair.

'Goodbye, Félix.'

'You *know* you love me.'

Standing up I crossed the street.

'Judith!'

From the other side of the rue de Buci, almost running, I looked round as Félix hurled some money into the ashtray.

'Wait, Judith!'

I pushed my way past the tourists clutching bottles of mineral water, the hunchback with his shopping basket, the rollerbladers, and two blue-shirted gendarmes with their pistols who were salivating in front of the chocolate-filled window of the *bonbonnerie*, towards the rue St Benoit where I had left the car.

'Judith! Come back.'

We were in the rue de l'Abbaye, separated by the traffic, by the drivers hurrying to get home. Félix was running along the sidewalk, struggling to reach me.

'You do love me Judith!' I saw him look to right and left before launching himself in front of a delivery van which braked sharply.

'No!'

I was impervious to the curious heads turning. Eluding him, I dived into the *passage privé* past the Indiana Café, the toyshop with its leering teddies and the Pedicures Medicales, twisting my ankle on the cobbles and losing myself in the crowds.

'No,' I yelled. '*No!*'

Had I not stopped at a bar, standing at the zinc in my black and white dress, oblivious to the predatory glances of the perched male conspiracy ostensibly watching football on TV, I might have remembered the memo-recorder sooner and that I had to get to it before Jordan. It had completely slipped my mind.

★   ★   ★

I seethed and cursed in the already gridlocked traffic crawling towards the river as a giant truck blocked the road. The strike was over and the garbage men were gathering up the black bags, shouting obscenities at each other, taking their time. Glancing at the cheery little icon on the dash, I saw that it registered empty and that in my delirium at going to Félix I had forgotten to fill the tank. Frantic and sweating in the sardine tin that was the Renault, I was afraid that I would run out of gas. I was making minuscule headway when a seemingly endless procession of nuns in grey habits, hands folded sedately before them, crossed the road in front of me. I was wondering were they trying to tell me something, when I realized that, in accordance with sod's law of which I seemed to have fallen inextricably foul, the rue de Seine, my shortest route, was temporarily *barrée*. Joining the long line for the deviation which would take me round the one-way system, I prayed that Jordan was not yet home.

By the time I reached the Boulevard Courcelles the cars were bumper to bumper and there was nowhere to park. Recklessly abandoning the Renault on the sidewalk and with my skirt cleaving to my legs, I ran the length of the street to find that the elevator, which always chose its moments, was *en panne* and that I would have to run up the five flights of stairs.

In the apartment Joey, damp and smelling

of chlorine, was in the hallway playing happily with his remote control car. He struggled to escape from the relieved embrace in which I encircled him, unable to separate his image from that of the boy, lying in the pool of his own blood, clutching his baguette.

'Let me go, Mom.'

That was the one thing I could not do.

Jordan was in the bedroom incandescent with triumph. When he saw me, out of breath and dishevelled, my face stained with tears, he looked at me oddly. The memo-recorder was no longer by the bed. I stood by the door in my crumpled black and white dress in horror, waiting for what was to come. Jordan stared at me for a long moment.

'Nadine said you'd gone to the coiffeuse.'

I put a hand to my dishevelled hair which tumbled from Michelle's Alice band.

'The hairdresser was closed.'

From the bathroom, while he was showering, his tongue loosened by the champagne with which he had been celebrating, Jordan related the events of his day. How the Viscomte had telephoned at one minute to twelve as the courier was impatiently waiting, how the French Government, whose reputation was at stake, had finally backed down. How the Rochelle Eléctronique deal would be safely signed, sealed and delivered in a few days at which point we would be going back to Boston. If he had listened to his memo-recorder, for which I searched frantically while he was in the shower but which I could not find, nothing was said, and I put his over-the-top behaviour — he was full of wild and uncharacteristic bonhomie — down to the champagne.

I don't know how I managed to smile through the iced soup and the gigot amid the vociferous sea of jubilant men in their shirt-sleeves (Jordan had insisted that they remove their coats) who surreptitiously wiped the perspiration from their foreheads as they raised excited glasses to the man of the moment, to Rochelle Eléctronique, to Cavendish Holdings and to Pilcher Bain.

In the dark oak dining-room I sat at the head of the table in my green Givenchy dress, my emerald earrings, my hair knotted tight on my head, making conversation to an expansive Claude Lafarge who had managed to lean on the Viscomte de Loisy and having persuaded him, during the course of several meetings, to withdraw the golden share clause, had apparently saved the day. He waxed lyrical about Jordan's tough and uncompromising strategy and insisted I drink a toast to my husband who — blind to the fact that my heart was breaking — impassively met my eyes over the blatant arrangement of red roses Nadine had innocently placed on the table.

With the *pièce de résistance*, carried in by the chef herself in a spotless white tunic, came a dramatic flash of lightning, then the room darkened and the curtains flapped angrily at the open windows. As she triumphantly set the overblown soufflé ('you can't hurry a soufflé') on the mahogany buffet, there was a deafening clap of thunder and the rain, for which we had been waiting for weeks, finally fell, putting an end to the long hot summer.

★　★　★

Coffee was served in the salon where Jordan plied his colleagues with Cognac and proffered cigars to the few who smoked. When the telephone rang in the hall I rushed to answer it.

Just the timbre of Félix's voice made me feel faint. Above the noise which emanated from the salon we could not be heard. Outside the rain was beating against the windows. I let him speak, let him tell him how much he loved me, how crucial I was to his life and how he was at a loss to comprehend why, after the intimacy we had created, an understanding so tender that everyone else was excluded, I had in a moment become alien, had stepped outside our charmed circle.

'I don't understand, Judith.' He said it over and over. 'I don't understand.'

How could I make him understand when I didn't understand myself why I had thrown away my chance of happiness, walked away from the garden of Eden.

'Listen carefully Félix . . . '

'You love me!' He wasn't listening. I pictured him in the studio, pacing up and down before my likeness, reclining on the daybed, testament to our love.

'I *thought* it was love. It was a romance. A summer romance.' Making my voice light, attempting to make it mocking, to make the situation less hard to bear, I listened to the rain beating against the windows. 'It was a wager,' I said. 'You won your bet. Go back to Olympe.' I turned the knife. 'The summer is over.'

In the salon, like the warriors of old, the men of finance were exchanging stories of derring-do. Jordan looked at me through the blue haze of smoke but he did not enquire who it was who had called.

It was after midnight when the last of the band departed. Unwilling to bring the evening to an end, Sherman stayed behind to

266

chew over the victory when the others had made their inebriated way to the elevator.

'A wonderful dinner, Judith.'

'Thank Nadine. I had nothing to do with it.'

'What do you think of your husband?'

I did not think. I could not think. It was as if I were paralysed and another Judith was thinking, moving, going through the motions of putting the room to rights, emptying the ashtrays for me.

'He'll be on the board in no time,' Sherman put an affectionate arm round his friend. 'That scheme he came up with was nothing short of masterly. He would have gone ahead with it too. Doesn't like being double-crossed. Do you know what this man here was doing while he was waiting for the Viscomte to telephone and we were all chewing our fingernails. Practising his putting! For Chrissakes, our future was on the line and he was practising his putting. You've got one hell of a cool husband. Are you looking forward to going home, Judith? Nadine can't wait.'

Lumping me together with Nadine, Sherman didn't wait for an answer. Devoted to love but unable to commit himself, women for him were not thinking, feeling human beings but indifferent objects existing only to satisfy the desires he was unable to control.

There are those who argue that 'love' does not exist, that it is a linguistic construct which provides the excuse for social, literary and political con tricks, that it is a state of physical and psychological arousal on which we confer the name of Eros while deluding ourselves with illusory grandeurs. Sick with love, yearning for Félix, my heart fragmented. I could not accept that the days of wine and roses were over and, unlike Nadine, I was not looking forward to going back to what I doubted would ever again seem like 'home'. I did not even know if, forced to become one person again after being two, I would have the strength to leave Paris.

When Sherman finally departed, I made myself busy in the kitchen although the caterers had left the place spotless and had spirited away the leftover food, and there was nothing for me to do except stare unseeingly as the Black Mollys and the guppies swum back and forth mindlessly in Joey's fish-tank.

I could not believe that in three days I would be going to back to my life in Boston, to taking care of the laundry and feeding the dog and making blueberry muffins for the school bake sale; that I would never again see the rue de Buci, the transvestite on his heels, the hunchback with his *panier*, and that the pinnacle of my week would be going out for a pizza with Nadine and Sherman rather than cracking leisurely crab claws *face à face* with my lover at a table for two in the Place de Clichy.

'I can hardly believe it's over,' Jordan said when, unable to procrastinate any longer, I finally went into the bedroom. High on the adrenalin of his success, he was not looking the least tired.

I listened, undressing slowly, while he recounted in exuberant detail the exact sequence of events at Pilcher Bain as he and his team waited to know the outcome of Rochelle Eléctronique.

'It could so easily have gone the other way,' Jordan said. 'It might well have done had it not been for Claude Lafarge.'

Sitting at the dressing-table, I brushed my hair remembering how Félix had brushed it, slowly, tenderly, and listened to Jordan holding forth about earnings before interest, tax, depreciation and amortisation, and future takeover opportunities — subjects dear to his heart. As the early morning cars hissed along the Boulevard Courcelles, I climbed reluctantly into the *lit-bateau*, dreading what might come.

'How was your day?' Jordan said as he removed his Rolex, checking its face automatically with the bedside clock which told the time on two continents. I wondered was he testing me, playing a game with me as he had played a game with the Viscomte de Loisy. Had he listened to my message on the memo-recorder and was he taking me to the edge? His voice was equable as usual, revealing nothing. A skilled poker player — he and Sherman had a regular game — Jordan never revealed his hand.

Was it only eight hours ago that I was contemplating leaving him and never going back to Boston. Lauren had been wrong. I would not miss the gym and the Museum of Fine Arts; I would not miss my jobette and my colleagues and I certainly wouldn't miss my dried-up stick of a mother-in-law. Delaying the moment, I rearranged the books on my bedside, the *Sonnets from the Portuguese* Félix had given me, the untouched bottle of pills prescribed by Dr Katz, and lay down on the square linen pillows with their borders of yellowing lace. Turning out the lamp I felt the warmth of Jordan's body permeate mine, then heard his heavy breathing. Knocked out by the champagne, exhausted by his triumphant day, he was asleep.

22

I hate airports. Like God's ante-room. I suppose because I don't like flying and am surprised every time the plane that I am travelling on makes a safe landing. It always amazes me that among the myriad faces of every age, every hue, every ethnic persuasion milling hither and thither, arriving and departing, no two are the same. The Flatlands, having checked in their mini-Everest of baggage, made a nervous little group outside the departure gate. Jordan, the conquering hero with his invisible wreath of laurels, anxious to wipe the dust of Paris from his feet and champing at the bit to get back to Boston; Michelle with her curled lip, on her mobile phone to Lois and standing, with her back to me, as far away as possible; Helga, rendered more useless than usual by the lure of Bananafanna Sundaes; Lauren, good old Lauren, who had come to see us off, to make sure that I got on the plane; and Joey, for whom we were all waiting, who had dashed off to buy a comic although Jordan had told him a dozen times to wait until we were through departure.

Packing was not my favourite occupation at the best of times, but ridding the apartment in the Boulevard Courcelles of the Flatland presence constituted a Sisyphean task as each suitcase was filled, each scarlet strap — Jordan insisted on easy identification — fastened over the well-worn valises, took me further away from Félix. Had it not been for Lauren I doubt I would have made it.

Coming into the apartment to see if there was anything she could do to help, she had found me sitting inert on the bed, surrounded by piles of garments prised from the heavy armoires, the cumbersome drawers, with tears running down my face.

'Why are you crying?'

'I'm not crying, I'm weeping.'

'Crying, weeping . . . Come on now, honey, everything's going to be all right.'

It was the sort of platitude you uttered to one bereaved. It was as if someone had died, as if I had been abandoned, although paradoxically it was I who had done the abandoning. Aristophanes had been right in describing the search by each half of the original double-being for the other. He had touched a nerve that still quivered, inspiring images of something lost, some longed-for wholeness from which I had unaccountably walked away. The pain was insupportable and the past few days, in which there had been no word from Félix, had been filled with a kaleidoscope of conflicting emotions, depression and despair.

'Look upon it as an illness,' Lauren said. 'You have to give yourself time to recover. Convalescence can last a long while. It can be painful.'

Love does not go away for the asking. I doubted if recovery would occur at all. Three times in the past few days, unable to help myself, I had telephoned Félix needing, like a shot on which I had become dependent, to hear his voice. Twice there had been no reply and I imagined the telephone ringing and ringing in the studio with its easel — had he removed my picture? — its mug of sharpened pencils, its wooden case of paints. On the third occasion a woman had answered — Olympe? — and I had slammed down the phone. Each time the telephone rang in the apartment I had rushed to answer it. It was for Michelle, for Helga, for Joey, the agent about the electricity and the gas. I had hardly seen Jordan who together with his team was busy finalizing the Rochelle Eléctronique contracts. When our paths did cross it was to discuss the nuts and bolts of leaving and the travel arrangements. At night he had been too tired, or too distracted to make love.

'You will get over it,' Lauren said. 'I've been there, honey. I know.'

How could I tell Lauren that her litany of men barely qualified as lovers. Although Lauren was my friend she was totally unable to understand that my passion for Félix was destroying me and that while one part of Judith Flatland was packing her shirts and her shoes, the other was craving to sit with Félix beneath an alley of clipped limes in the Luxembourg Gardens, to spend a leisurely day amongst the Picassos in the Marais, to pass a darkened afternoon in the womb of the *cinématèque*, to listen to the clickety-click of the turnstiles in the métro, to stroll arm in arm around the Paris of Corneille and Rossini, of Balzac and Delacroix, of James Joyce, Hemingway and Scott Fitzgerald, towards the cool of his studio where love would come first and, after love, talk and, after talk a visit to the Buci market.

'You made the right decision . . . ' Lauren picked up a skirt and folded it.

I snatched it from her hand.

'I didn't make the decision.'

It was made for me.

'I hate to see you like this, Judith. I wish I could do something.'

I knew that I was beyond assistance, that no one could save me from the cataclysm that had overtaken me, least of all myself. I had started to drink and made inroads into the whisky bottle in the buffet, rinsing my mouth out with mouthwash before Jordan was due home.

* * *

Jordan, family passports in his hand — he liked to be in control and didn't trust anybody with them — was looking impatiently at his Rolex, as we waited for Joey. He dispatched Helga to the bookstore to tell him to come immediately. I wondered, as I had wondered many times before, why airport jargon had to be so downbeat with its 'final calls' and 'terminals', as if we were all doomed. I had just scanned the 'departures' screen, in the vain hope that the flight to Boston had been cancelled and was about to check my hand baggage for the umpteenth time — candy and his Game Boy for Joey, books and a sweater for myself — when I noticed the red rose at my feet.

Lauren was busy talking to Jordan, and Michelle had wandered off after Helga, as my eyes scanned the passing crowds with their dilatory children and their warm coats for colder climes and their suitcases on wheels.

When I caught sight of Félix through the

open front of the parfumerie, I was turned to stone.

'I won't be long,'

'Not now, Judith,' Jordan said, as the blood once more began to flow. 'We're late as it is. They'll be calling the flight any minute.'

'I forgot your mother's eau de Cologne.'

I abandoned my hand baggage and the agony of the past few days and flew across the concourse towards the pink fasciaed boutique with its opaque shelves of *Arpège*, and *Vol de Nuit*, and *Egoïste*, and *Fleur d'Interdit* for little girls.

He was standing, in his black shirt and black trousers, among the seductive display of designer bottles and outsize flasks. His eyes were red and his chin stubbled and he looked as if he had not slept for days.

'You lied to me Judith . . . ' I had never seen him angry.

'No.'

I shook my head at a smiling pink acolyte who offered to envelop me in a free cloud of *Opium*, as I made my way to his side.

'You lied . . . '

Heads, testing essences and tying ribbons, were turned as he raised his voice.

'Tell me the truth.'

I thought that he was going to hit me, but he grabbed my arm.

'Félix, please . . . ' I lowered my voice encouraging him to do the same. 'People are looking.'

'*Tant pis.*'

A French voice came over the public address system. The message was repeated in fractured English:

'TWA flight 262 for Boston — '

'They're calling my flight!'

' — immediate boarding. Gate number three.'

'Félix, I have to go.'

'You're not going anywhere.'

'Jordan is waiting. I'm going to miss the plane.'

It was a full moment, during which the last-minute purchasers melted away, the serried ranks of distinctive boxes disappeared from sight and I was alone with Félix, before I realized that although he had released my arm, like Pygmalion, I was unable to move.

'One minute, Judith. *One* minute.'

He drew me to him. I did not respond. Over his shoulder, behind the counter, I could see the stainless-steel clock with its stainless-steel hand calibrating the seconds.

Body to body in the fragrant grotto, my own immobile, I could feel his blood coursing through my veins as his mouth covered mine and the sixty segments of the one minute he had demanded of me were consumed in jerky strokes. There were five seconds left when I felt the wave hit and was carried away by the familiarity of the wall of water against which I was defenceless.

'*Dis le*, Judith.' The words were no louder than a caress. 'Let me hear you say it.'

' . . . final call for flight number 262 for Boston . . . '

Jordan would be beside himself. I looked at Félix.

'*Excusez-moi!*' We were in the way. People, clutching their pale pink plastic carriers bearing the logo of the parfumerie, were trying to get by.

'I love you.' I loved him. 'I love you. *Je t'aime*, Félix. *Que je t'aime*.'

'*Mon amour*.' His arms were round me, sapping my strength.

'Mom . . . ' I hadn't seen Michelle approach. I realized that she was not only addressing me but that her voice was gentle. Prising myself loose from Félix's arms, and without looking back, I followed my daughter out of the store.

★　★　★

I sat in the aisle seat. Jordan liked to sit by the window. In an ideal world he would have liked to fly the plane. I presumed that Joey had reappeared from the bookstore with the comic he was devouring in the seat in front of us, that our hand baggage had passed through the X-ray machines, that we had presented ourselves, in the nick of time, with our boarding passes at the appropriately numbered gate and that, despite all the alarums and excursions, we had actually made our flight, because we appeared to have not only to have taken off but to be suspended high above the clouds.

The flight attendant, in her red uniform, her long fingernails painted to match, was demonstrating the safety instructions:

'Your life vest is stowed under your seat. When directed to do so by the crew, remove your life vest from its container and pull it over your head . . . '

A tear coursed down my face. This time I was crying. Looking in the hand baggage for a Kleenex, I found the plastic snowstorm and watched, mesmerized, as the tormented white flakes settled round the Eiffel Tower before replacing it in the bag.

Joey took his innocent blond head out of his comic.

'What's green and goes up and down, Mom?'

'Pull the tapes down, passing them around

your waist and fastening them securely in a double bow at the side . . . '

'I have no idea, Joey. What is green and goes up and down?'

'A gooseberry in a lift!'

'In your seat pocket there is a card which contains details of the escape routes . . . '

Across the aisle, Michelle was talking animatedly to a broad-shouldered young man in the seat next to her. Helga, masticating a stick of gum, was stowing Joey's belongings.

'The emergency exits are on both sides of the aircraft . . . ' The scarlet-tipped fingers were extended, back and front and side to side. 'They are clearly marked.'

There was a ping as the warning signs were extinguished. Jordan released his seat belt and opened the briefcase on his lap. Inside it, beneath a photograph of himself, the headline in the *Wall Street Journal* read:

'Golden Share Waiver.
Pilcher Bain Clinch Merger.'

Beside the newspaper, on top of his neatly stacked papers, was his memo-recorder. Our eyes met and I saw him for the first time in weeks. Making no comment on the fact that I was crying, he put an arm around me. The Flatlands were going home.

We do hope that you have enjoyed reading this large print book.

Did you know that all of our titles are available for purchase?

We publish a wide range of high quality large print books including:
Romances, Mysteries, Classics
General Fiction
Non Fiction and Westerns

Special interest titles available in large print are:
The Little Oxford Dictionary
Music Book
Song Book
Hymn Book
Service Book

Also available from us courtesy of Oxford University Press:
Young Readers' Dictionary
(large print edition)
Young Readers' Thesaurus
(large print edition)

For further information or a free brochure, please contact us at:
Ulverscroft Large Print Books Ltd.,
The Green, Bradgate Road, Anstey,
Leicester, LE7 7FU, England.
Tel: (00 44) 0116 236 4325
Fax: (00 44) 0116 234 0205

Other titles published by
The House of Ulverscroft:

THE LONG HOT SUMMER

Rosemary Friedman

A precise, elegant and witty novel. Lorna Brown had everything . . . wall-to-wall carpets, au pairs, clothes, en suite bathrooms.. so what is ailing her? How could she explain to her husband? Lorna welcomes the diversion provided by Armand, a contemporary of her daughter's. And in a sudden decision walks away from her life in Home Farm Close to a squat in Regent's Park.

FRESH AS A DAISY

Valerie-Anne Baglietto

Daisy's feet have barely touched the ground since marrying Ben Kavanagh after a passionate, whirlwind romance. But she's soon brought down to earth with a bump when she meets her in-laws in their impressive Jacobean manor house. Ben's father and stepmother are suspicious of her motives, and she instantly feels like an outsider. As the bloom fades from her marriage, Daisy finds herself turning to the charming and enigmatic Jerome. But when her past comes back to confront her, she realises she's not the only one harbouring a secret or two.

THE BEST-KEPT SECRET

Mary De Laszlo

Cornelia, an innocent seventeen-year-old, is to leave the sheltered atmosphere of her Catholic boarding school and spend a year in Paris. First, though, she must meet the redoubtable Aunt Flavia, who proceeds to transform the schoolgirl into a beautifully presented young woman. Next it is school at Mademoiselle Beatrice's, where Cornelia meets other English girls, most of whom are just as naive as she is. Then there is Laurent, without whom Paris would never be Paris. So begins the happy initiation which will change her life forever.

HIS 'N' HERS

Mike Gayle

From their first meeting at the student union over a decade ago, Jim and Alison successfully navigated their way through first dates, meeting parents, moving in together and more . . . Then they split up and divided their worldly goods (including a sofa, a cat and their flat) into his 'n' hers. Now, three years on and with new lives and new loves, they couldn't be happier — until a chance encounter throws them back together, and causes them to embark on a journey through their past to ask themselves the big question: where did it all go wrong and is it too late to put it all right?

FOR MATRIMONIAL PURPOSES

Kavita Daswani

'Who needs you to be happy? I want to see you married this year.' This is the view of Anju's mother, in the time-honoured tradition of all mothers, but particularly that of the fond Indian parent. Anju now works in New York, living the sophisticated American lifestyle — almost. But when she returns home to her parents in Bombay — usually for another family wedding — she finds herself reverting to the traditional daughter role. At each visit another prospective suitor is brought forward. But what sort of man does the very modern Anju want? How important are her family, her country, her traditions?